For Aidan,

Happy Birthday October 2002

love Grandma Nels

WALTER MACKEN, author and dramatist, was born in Galway in 1916. At seventeen he began writing plays and joined the celebrated Irish-language Taibhdhearc Theatre as an actor. In 1936 he married and moved to London for two years, returning to become actor-manager-director of the Taibhdhearc for nine years, during which time he produced many successful translations of plays by Ibsen, Shaw, O'Casey, Capek and Shakespeare. He moved to the Abbey Theatre in Dublin, and later acted on the London stage, on Broadway, and took a leading part in the film of Brendan Behan's *The Quare Fellow*. Many of his plays have been published, and of his early novels *I Am Alone* (1948) and *Rain on the Wind* (1949) were initially banned in Ireland. Several other novels followed including *The Bogman*, which first appeared in 1952, and a historical trilogy on Ireland, *Seek the Fair Land, The Silent People* and *The Scorching Wind*. Two collections of short stories, *God Made Sunday* and *The Green Hills*, won considerable critical acclaim on both sides of the Atlantic. His last work, *Brown Lord of the Mountain*, was published just a month before his death in 1967.

WALTER
MACKEN
The Green Hills
AND OTHER STORIES

BRANDON

Published in 1996 by
Brandon Book Publishers Ltd.
Dingle, Co. Kerry, Ireland.

Copyright © Walter Macken 1962

British Library Cataloguing in Publication Data is
available for this book.

ISBN 0 86322 216 1

Brandon receives financial assistance from the Arts Council/
An Chomhairle Ealaíon, Ireland

Cover illustration: Steven Hope
Typesetting: Koinonia, Bury
Printed by The Guernsey Press, Channel Islands

Contents

Contents

Gaeglers and the Wild Geese

IT WAS ONLY a man of exceptional daring who would face Bulger after — let's use the right spade word — robbing him. Because it was robbery whatever way you look at it, and afterward Bulger lay awake many a long night thinking about it, and fulminating, and imagining his huge, beefy hands wrapped around Gaeglers' neck and seeing his swollen tongue emerging from his throttle while he, Bulger, laughed at his popping eyes. But then, Gaeglers was an exceptional man.

It happened very simply. Gaeglers and a friend were walking along in a town in the West of Ireland one September morning, and the friend said that he would dearly love a drink, that his tongue was hanging out, and how would he get one? Gaeglers confessed that he had no money at the moment and said he was sorry for his friend. The friend was surprised Gaeglers had no money, because he was rarely without it. He looked prosperous, too, in a nice blue suit and a white shirt with an open collar. He never wore a tie, winter or summer, and he always looked good, with his dark complexion and tight curly hair. His shoes always shone and his trousers were always creased. He didn't work at anything specific that anybody could see, and people who had to earn a living viewed his immaculate appearance with an indignant eye. Gaeglers said he was a factor.

Just then, they came level with a small shop that had been recently opened by Bulger, where he sold vegetables and fish and fowl. The stuff was all stacked neatly on shelves or hanging from hooks. All very clean and hygienic – and obviously the shop was due to be successful. Bulger was a newcomer to the town – a countryman. He was very big. His feet were big and his body was big, and the white linen coat he wore seemed to make him even bigger, but he had a very friendly smile, and all the poorer ladies, who wore shawls and had to bargain everywhere for their food, knew that they could always get a halfpenny off a herring from Bulger on a Friday.

"Excuse me now a moment," said Gaeglers to his friend, and turned and went into the little shop.

There was a lady buying a hen, so he waited politely while she probed the animal. If she had been a surgeon, she couldn't have given the hen a better biological examination, Gaeglers thought. She did everything but ask for a birth certificate. Bulger was very patient, and pointed out the hen's good points and explained that it was a boiling fowl and not a one for the oven; he concealed nothing about the hen's origin and finally effected a sale.

"Some of them are tough," he said to Gaeglers with a smile when she had gone.

"The hens or the dames?" Gaeglers asked.

Bulger was examining him curiously. Gaeglers knew from the look in Bulger's eyes that he recognized him and had heard talk about him and that the proposition he was about to make would come as no surprise. He dramatised it a bit on that account, looking swiftly here and there, and then more or less speaking with his lips closed. "Like a salmon or two?" he asked, and watched the thoughts on the honest countenance.

Bulger's thoughts were clear. He wanted salmon. They would not be legitimate salmon but poached ones; therefore their price would be lower and his profit bigger, and he had many customers clamouring for them, because they were scarce. He fell to the dishonest temptation with a sigh. "I might," he said. "How much?"

"Very special," said Gaeglers. "Three bob a pound." This was a third of the price prevailing for the legitimates.

"All right," Bulger said.

"You give me a pound note," said Gaeglers. "A gesture of good faith for the – eh – fishermen, and you can pay the rest on delivery."

Bulger handed over a pound.

Gaeglers pocketed it, and then joined his friend and said, "We will go and have a drink now, my friend. There's a sucker born every minute."

Bulger is still waiting for his salmon.

Gaeglers went back, all right. He paid Bulger a call every Friday and bought three or four herrings to take home for dinner. If Gaeglers talked at all in the busy shop, he always brought in the word "honesty." He had good fun for a long time with Bulger, watching the blood mounting in his face and seeing the big fists clenching. Bulger couldn't attack him in front of the customers. If he wished, he could go to the police and tell them that he had been defrauded over buying illicit salmon.

One Friday in December, Gaeglers paid his weekly call looking for herrings. There was a tall man in the shop. He had three large feathered animals hanging from each hand. He put them on the counter. Bulger went to the cashbox and took out a lot of notes. He handed them over to the tall man.

"Eighteen pounds," said Bulger, "and not a penny more."

"Three pounds each is not much," said the man.

"I wish I could get my money as easy," said Bulger.

Gaeglers was interested. "What kind of ducks are those?" he asked.

The man laughed. "Them's not ducks," he said. "They're wild geese."

"Do they lay gold eggs?" Gaeglers asked. "Or what?"

The man laughed. "Goodbye," he said to Bulger, and went out.

Gaeglers followed him. He didn't even wait to buy the herrings. "Could we go and have a drink?" he asked the man, who was stowing away the notes.

"We could," said the man. "Why not?"

He was taller than Gaeglers. His face was very tanned. He smelled of turf and heather and things like that. He had a slow, loping walk. "Call me Tom," he said. They went into a pub.

"I'm interested in those birds," said Gaeglers. "I never thought that you could sell one of those birds for that much money. How much does it cost you to rear them?"

Tom laughed again. "Man, you're a caution!" he exclaimed. "You don't rear them. You shoot them. They're wild geese. Do you know how much those six birds cost me?"

"How much?"

"Fourpence halfpenny," said the man. "The price of one cartridge. I got the six of them with the one shot."

Gaeglers added up in his mind. He thought that the profits were fabulous. It was a source of income to be tapped and he had never even heard about it. "Is it difficult to shoot them?" he asked.

"Naw," Tom said. "You just cross a bit of bog to a lonely mountain lake, sit down on your fanny, wait until they light on the water, and then let them have it." He knocked off a pint of beer, hardly moving his Adam's apple.

Gaeglers was impressed. "I'm very interested in this," he said. "The next time you are going after these birds, would it be possible for me to go with you?"

Tom looked Gaeglers up and down. "You could come," he said. "It's a bit lonely on your own. I'd be glad of company. If we kill a lot, you could have a share. How's that?"

"That's fine," said Gaeglers. "Have another pint." He was thinking hard. If this fellow could get eighteen pounds for six geese, how many could Gaeglers get for twenty? It would set him up all winter. If you could get six geese with one cartridge fired from a shotgun, how many could you get if you could borrow a cannon? The thing was to get to know the ground and then decide on tactics. He would have to go out into the country, he supposed. Gaeglers didn't like the country. The nearest he wanted to get to the country was a bench in the park in the town, where he could read the racing results in the sun. Still, if a thing like this could be organized, it could mean a lot.

So one morning about a week later, Gaeglers alighted from a bus in the street of a small village and shivered. He was wearing a lightweight blue suit and an open-necked white shirt and thin shoes with pointed toes. The sun was shining coldly outside the bus. Inside, behind the sheltering glass, it had seemed almost hot.

Tom was there. Gaeglers winced at his handclasp. Tom shook his head when he had looked him over. "Will you be cold on the mountain in them clothes?" he asked.

Gaeglers slapped his chest. "Not me," he boasted. "I'm the warmest-blooded man in the twenty-six counties. Lead me to those geese."

"All right," said Tom. "We'll go after the geese."

They called at Tom's house to collect the guns. He gave Gaeglers a single-barrelled gun that he had borrowed. His own was double-barrelled, old and well cared for. Gaeglers hefted his gun. He thought it was light. He threw it in the air and caught it on the way down. It was after midday when they set out. There was a gently sloping mountain at the back of the house, covered with faded heather and sedge. It looked solid and yellow.

"We just have to climb up there and beyond a bit to the lake," Tom said.

"That's the stuff," said Gaeglers.

"It will be dark by four," Tom said, "so they should be flighting a bit before that."

First they walked along a dirt road that had been made so people could bring down their turf from the bogs. That was all right. It was firm and good underfoot, even though Gaeglers could feel some of the stones trying to rip through the soles of his thin shoes. The road faded away then, and they had to take to the side of the mountain.

At once, one of Gaeglers' feet went into soft bog and he felt the water in his shoe. He howled and tried to pull back, and the other shoe went bogging as well.

Tom hauled him out. "Keep off the soft bits," he advised. "Come after me and walk where I walk."

Gaeglers was cursing vividly. The water in his shoes was cold. Tom wore rubber boots that came nearly to his knees. Gaeglers walked in Tom's steps, but it was like walking into a little pool each time. His socks were squelching. He cursed and then took to jumping from tussock to tussock. Sometimes he missed a tussock and the weight of the jump sank his legs to the shin in brown slime.

It was a grand day. The sky was steel blue. The wind was from the north. Some of the bog pools had a thin sheeting of ice. Gaeglers didn't notice those things. The song of the bog lark meant nothing to him. He was unhappy. He was sweating. The gentle slope of the mountain was gentle only from a distance. It seemed to Gaeglers that it was a perpendicular cliff now. Tom was ahead, walking easily with a free-swinging stride. Gaeglers was trying to keep up with him. There was a band across his chest, and every now and again he had to cough. His mouth was dry. His tongue seemed to be hanging out on his chin. He let his feet go where they willed. He became used to the squelching in his shoes. All he wanted was that the pilgrimage should come to an end. He could have called out and begged Tom to stop and rest, but pride wouldn't let him admit that a man he regarded as an inferior country gob could do something he couldn't do.

After an hour, Tom stopped and rested on an outcropping of rock. Gaeglers laboured up to him. His lungs seemed to have shrunk; they couldn't get enough air. The light gun he was carrying seemed as heavy as two hundredweight of coal. He sat down, trying to hide the short breaths he was being forced to take, and blinking his eyes to shut out the spots dancing in front of them.

Tom was nonchalantly lighting a pipe. His breathing was even. "We'll be there in about another hour," he said.

Gaeglers wanted to die.

Tom was leaning on his elbow. "It's worth the little walk up here to look at that view," he was saying. "Man, it's powerful." He carefully kept his eyes away from the pitiful wretch beside him. You sweat when you climb, but when you sit down on the side of a mountain in a north wind, the wind soon dries the sweat and then explores every opening in your clothes. Gaeglers shivered. He might as well have been dressed in light cotton as the suit he wore, and his two feet in the sodden, destroyed shoes were like two blocks of ice. The steel of the gun was sticking to his shivering hand.

"We'll go now," Gaeglers practically begged.

"Begod," said Tom, rising. "You're a great man on a mountain."

So I have fooled the bastard, Gaeglers thought.

The hour was a long one. Every fold of the mountain seemed to be the top, but beyond it there would be another fold; eventually they reached the top and looked down on the sheet of lake in the valley. Gaeglers stumbled down to it behind Tom, trying to figure out how he had got into this thing. It was the sight of the crinkling notes being handed over for a few feathered animals. That was it. Otherwise it would never have struck him. Great God, give him back a few days of his life and avarice would never again be one of his sins.

There was a deep cut in a bank near the lake. Tom put him in there. But first he showed him the reed roots along the shore that had been pulled up by the geese, and he showed him the feathers on the ground.

"The thing to do is to let them land," Tom said. "Don't move a muscle or blink an eye when you hear them coming in. Just let them land, and when they are nicely bunched on the water, let them have it. I'll go over the far side, and when they take off into the wind, I may get a crack at them."

Gaeglers could only nod a reply, and then Tom was gone.

Gaeglers closed his eyes. He had never been so utterly exhausted in his life. He slept. The cold woke him. The sun was lower in the sky, and the wind was whistling in the heather where he sheltered. His body was racked with bouts of shivering. He had to clench his jaws to keep his teeth from chattering. He felt light in the head. He tried to bury himself deeper in the cleft. The ground was wet where his body rested. He should be in the snug of a pub in the town, warm and comforted in a smog made up of smoke and the fumes of porter. It was the first time in his life that he had ever made a mistake. It better be worth it, this mistake. He tried to think of twenty birds at three pounds each. Sixty pounds. That would be worth this agony.

The sun was gone almost entirely when a distant honking sounded in the sky. The geese came in, in V formation, from the crab-apple-green sunset and then swung wide and came from behind him, so as to land against the wind. His heart was pounding. He waited, and there was a frightening swishing of wings over his head and a great rustling and splashing as thirty big bodies hit the water in a little bay right in front of his eyes.

He raised the gun to his shoulder and sighted it and pulled the trigger. Nothing happened. He stood up, cursing and wrenching at the thing. He had forgotten to take off the safety catch. There was a frightened honking from the geese as he stood there, and then they rose from the water, their great wings spread, and seemed to shoot straight up into the air like rockets. He fired the gun. It made a loud bang. He waited to hear bodies hitting the water.

The great flight drew together, going higher and higher, honking indignantly, and then they swung away to the other side of the world. They were all alive. They were all healthy.

Tom came over to him. "Too bad," he said. "They never came near me. I couldn't get a shot at them at all."

Gaeglers was practically crying. "All that – for nothing," he said. "All that for nothing."

"Maybe the next time," said Tom consolingly.

If there had been a cartridge in the gun, Gaeglers might have shot him.

He followed Tom up and then, finally, down the mountain. At least, he thought miserably, going down a mountain is easier than coming up a mountain. It might have been if there had been a moon. But there was no moon. He fell several times. Once, his chin hit the gun, the skin split, and he bled profusely over his clothes.

Near the place where the road should be, he saw Tom's bulk in front of him, and then the ground seemed very soft under Gaeglers and he slid gently into a boghole. It was a good thing he couldn't have seen, by day, the green slime covering it. He tasted it now as the water closed over him. He thrashed with his arms and his head came out of it and he shouted. He felt strong arms pulling at him, and then he stood there. He was bereft of even blasphemy.

Tom said a strange thing. "I didn't mean that," he said.

Gaeglers couldn't appreciate it then. They tried to squeeze some of the slime from his hair and the worst of it from his clothes.

Tom put him into the bus. The conductor took a poor view of his going home in the bus at all.

Tom talked to him through the window. "Listen, Gaeglers," he said. "Something you should know. I'm Bulger's brother. You shouldn't have swindled Bulger. Wild geese are really only worth a pound each. Good night." And then he was gone.

Gaeglers thought about it. He thought about it for a long time, and he came to an inane conclusion. It was a terrible expensive pound, Gaeglers concluded.

The Currach Race

————◇————

IT ALL DEVELOPED from Colm's visit to Sorcha's house
on the eve of St Patrick's Day.

He knew that he was not really welcome there. Welcome
to Sorcha, and welcome to her mother Siobhan, and to her
young brother Fintan, but the principal person in the house,
Sorcha's father Donagh, was terribly polite to him, and
listened so carefully to all his opinions that Colm felt sweat
breaking out all over him. All the others combined with their
kindness and affection and good wishes towards him would
be almost completely ineffective against the disapproval of the
principal member.

He hadn't wanted to come to the house at all, but Sorcha
kept pressing him. You will have to face up to him, she said.
Let him see what you are and he will get to like you even
though you do not like the sea.

That was the trouble.

Their village faced into the Atlantic. Sometimes the
Atlantic smiled on them and sometimes it frowned, but the
people knew all its moods now, and they ploughed their
stony fields in times, and in times they took their currachs out
and ploughed the sea for fish, to augment their food supplies,
or to sell them to the avid men from the town within who
came in their lorries.

Colm was different. Colm didn't like the sea. He thought
it took too much for the little it gave, so he concentrated on
the stony fields. His father before him was the same. He
cleared his fields of the stones, and he manured them well,

and ploughed them and protected them with tough trees and high stone walls from the destruction of the salt-laden winds from the sea. Sometimes, then, when a family had died out, from emigration or from the quick, vicious and unexpected death that the Atlantic occasionally brought, Colm's father, and after him Colm would buy the empty holding and would patiently rip the stones from the fields with crowbars or sticks of gelignite, and would manure and plough and attend until, by the present time, they had a holding of twenty acres, not counting bogland and the grouseland of the low hills.

His place was a marvel, because it actually paid. He was the only man inside eight parishes of this townland to have a farm that grew sweetly and paid a return, without him ever wetting an oar in a wave. He laid his fields out in the high-priced vegetables that he sold in the town. He kept three cows with bursting udders. He sold their milk and the butter from their milk in the town. Colm prospered from the attended land, and with a grant from the Government he tore off the thatched roof of his house and built a slated roof in its place. He erected new stables too with asbestos roofing on them, and they were very warm and clean inside so that the cows were pleased with them in the cold Atlantic winters and gave him a good return.

So why should Donagh disapprove of him?

Colm tried to figure it out, sitting there in the wooden chair out from the open fireplace. He was a big man with large capable hands that he was wiping against each other now. He had a big face that was shaved clean and he had on a new navy blue suit with the tailor's crease still in it. Donagh was leaning back in his chair, one hobnailed foot resting on his knee. He was dressed in the coarse homespun trousers and the grey wool shirt and the white bainin coat. What was good enough for my father is good enough for me. He was sixty years and more of age, but he was long, lean and lithe, and only gave away his age in the temple grey of his wiry black hair and the few grey bristles of his unshaven face. His stomach was as flat as the top of a table; and although Colm knew he hadn't more than ten shillings in the blue jug on the dresser and wasn't likely to have in the future, all the same Colm felt that Donagh was a better man than he would ever be, and every line of the body of the man, every weather wrinkle on his brown face, said that thing over and over again.

Colm thought: Will I go away now altogether?

Then he looked over at Sorcha.

She was at the table by the dresser, drying the dishes for her mother. Her hair was black too, and it waved in an unruly fashion, and her skin was very clear. She was wearing a blue dress with white dots on it, that was belted to her narrow waist, and the way she was standing he could see the long shapely length of her thigh. Her eyes caught his and she seemed to be saying, Don't go away, and Colm realised how much he loved Sorcha; so he said, To hell with the oul divil, and sat straight in his chair and stopped rubbing his hands together.

"So you don't like boats, Mister Colm?" said Donagh, very politely.

"I didn't say I didn't like boats," said Colm, "I just said that there's too much time taken up with boats in the village. That's all I said. I like a boat now and again. I like to take a currach out on the sea of a Sunday and catch a few fat pollack on the long line and cook them for the supper, but I think that the more a man gives to his land the more he gets out of it and the more he gives to the sea the less he gets out of it, and if it doesn't kill him in the end, it drains the life out of him."

Now I'm done with, he thought, seeing the flash of dismay in Sorcha's eyes. I should have kept my big mouth shut. It's many the time a person's mouth broke his nose, but I'm not a hypocrite, and if Sorcha really was for me, she would choose between her own father and myself and be done with it. It wasn't that either. It was just that she loved her father and wouldn't hurt him, although how anybody could love the oul divil, I fail to see, Colm thought sourly.

"It wouldn't be that you'd be afraid of the boats, now, Mister Colm," Donagh went on, as polite as ever, like the blade of a sharp gutting knife. "You're the oddest man that ever was bred in this village if you are."

"It's just that we don't agree," said Colm, "and maybe now we better leave it there."

"Fair enough," said Donagh. "That's where we'll leave it. Would you come over to Kinneally's beyont now and we'll drink a glass of stout together, or do you be against stout-drinking too?"

"All right," said Colm, "I will go to Kinneally's with you." This is kiss goodbye now, he thought. He told Sorcha that he didn't like coming into her house. He never would be able to get around saying, Sorcha and mesel want to be married, Donagh, and she would like you to like it if you can. Everyone in the whole place knew about Sorcha and himself, even Donagh, but it would choke him to get the words out. So he didn't, and that was that and now they would have to seek another solution.

"We won't be long, Siobhan," Donagh was saying to his wife. "I'll be back in about half an hour." He emphasized the I'll. Sorcha's mother had a worried frown between her eyes. "All right, Donagh," she said. "Come back again sometime, Colm," she said. Make another effort to get on with Donagh.

"I'll walk ye to the road," said Sorcha, coming out the door after them and taking Colm's hand when they hit the moonlight outside. The hand farthest away from her father. She pressed it with her fingers and held the back of his hand for a moment against her thigh. Just a warm pressure of sympathy. That's a woman for you.

"Don't get drunk now let ye," she said standing near the

road and watching them away. It was a very brave night, frosty, with many stars and a fresh breeze that drove clouds like sheep across the face of the moon, so that it seemed to be racing and grinning down at them. Donagh stood there beside them, implacably, so that they couldn't talk. "Go back into the house now, girl," he said, "or you'll be catchin' cold."

"Good night," said Sorcha, and turned away.

Like two strangers they walked the half-mile to the pub. There was a three-foot space of dislike between them. Donagh was taller than Colm. He walked straighter. He had powerful shoulders. Colm was low but he was strong. Here's a fisherman and a farmer walking the road and for all the affinity they had they might as well have been engaged in their respective occupations.

Colm was glad when they left the frosty road for the smuggy yellow light of Kinneally's. It was full of men. There was a low counter and a few forms and half-barrels on which you could sit. There was the smell of porter and the guttering paraffin lamp and a fug of twist tobacco.

They were greeted. Donagh got a more fulsome greeting than Colm. Donagh insisted on paying for the two pints that were set up for them. Colm swallowed his slowly. Donagh downed his almost in a gulp. Colm ordered two more, paid for them from the small leather purse he carried in his pocket, and then he sat on a barrel and felt miserable and lonely, but never once wished he was a fisherman so that he could have Sorcha in the church without question and so that he would be able to laugh and be great friends of the men in Kinneally's pub.

He just sat there and thought and he didn't know what time it was that he took an interest in the conversation. Donagh was arguing with the Conneelys with old Kinneally behind the counter backing him up. What was it about? It was about boats. The two B's, Colm often thought before. They go together. Boats and boasting. The Conneelys were two brothers, twins in appearance, tall rangy men with great chests and unshaven chins. They were laughing at Donagh. We are the two finest men that ever went into a currach, they were saying. If you put Fionn Mac Cumhail and Goll Mac Morna and Cucullainn in a boat apart from us and if you tied the right arm to our sides we would give them a four mile lead and beat them home. They laughed, showing great white teeth in their dark faces, and they banged their pint glasses on the counter.

"The two a ye," Donagh was saying. "I'm an old man. I'm nearly double the age a ye. I could g' out on that bay tomorrow morning, if I had a child in the boat with me to balance it, and I could welt the two a ye. Is that right, Kinneally?"

"You were ever a powerful man in a boat," said Kinneally sincerely. "And your father before you was the same. If your father was alive, God rest him, and was in the seat with you in the same boat, there isn't two men in Ireland could whip ye."

"What?" asked James, the taller Conneely. "Is it poor oul Donagh? What man, days away he might have been good, but the salt has the meat eaten offa him now. He's fit for nothing better now but being a ghillie for stupid fishermen on an inshore lake."

Donagh was in a red rage. He cursed them. He called them names. They laughed at him. They were all a little drunk by this anyhow. All the men in the pub had closed around them and with sly grins were urging them on. Donagh was squaring up, as old men will do when their virility is questioned. He was hitching at his belt. There was a fire in his eye.

"Come on now!" he was saying. "Come on out now. Drag down yeer boats into the light of the moon and we'll launch them and I'll take on the two of ye."

"Ah, look now," Kinneally was saying, becoming a little afraid that things might get hot. "Cool off, men. There's tomorrow. Tomorrow is a holy holiday. Settle it tomorrow."

"I'll take them on tonight or tomorrow or any day in the

year," Donagh was shouting. "There wasn't a Conneely born yet that I couldn't bate blindfolded on the sea or the shore. I'll fight them now the two of them here on this spot, if they want it that way." He was pulling at his coat.

Colm must have been a little drunk too.

"Don't be an old fool, Donagh," he shouted over the din.

Donagh calmed down, hitched up his coat and turned slowly to face him.

"All right," he said. "Mister Colm tells me to calm down. I'm calm now, men. We'll make this fit. Here you have me, an old man. There you have two young men whose mouths are stronger than their hearts. We'll launch two currachs tomorrow after last Mass and we'll have a trial of strength across the bay. Them in one boat. Me in the other, and Colm here coming with me to balance it. He knows nothin' about boats, ye know. He doesn't approve of boats, ye know. So he can just sit on his tail coat and flip an oar, if there is that much good in him. And I'll still bate ye. Hear that now. Well, Mister Colm. What do you say to that now?"

Colm should have gone home. He realised that later. But the old man had him mad too.

"Maybe I can row a boat betther than any man here," he said. "Maybe I can now. Maybe I can show some of ye heroes that a farmer is a better man in a boat than any two of ye!" What has come over me? The things I despise. The two B's. Boasting and boats, and here I am in the middle of them all because an old man looks at me with scorn and derision and taunting in his eyes. I don't like him. This has nothing to do with his daughter. This is just something between him and me. They stood up straight and glared at each other, and Colm put down his glass and walked out of the place. He heard laughter following him into the night.

In a city, if two men come along and dig a hole in the street, they can gather an audience of thousands of people.

After last Mass on St Patrick's Day in the village there were hundreds of people gathered on the two necks of land which embraced the sea on either side of the strand. The whole place was shaped like a C lying down like this: ∩ . Six miles of rough sea separated the two arms. The sun was cold looking and there was a good breeze travelling from the direction of America. You would swear that the sea was clapping its hands, because somebody had told it there were four fools who might otherwise have remained out of its grip at this time of the year. The tips of the arms were rocky promontories, like two spear points of tested metal which dug into the waves and broke them up. They were festooned with people. There was colour there. All the lassies in their Sunday clothes and the old women in red petticoats and check aprons and plaid kerchiefs. The sun gleamed off the handlebars of bicycles lying grotesquely in the fields. They were chattering and laughing loudly and laying bets on the event.

Colm went through agonies of embarrassment as he made his way down to the south point. People made way for him and pointed him out. He felt cold in his stomach. He had given up wondering what had possessed him the night before, and he had come down here hoping that it was only a drunken dare and that he could go home and forget all about it. The sight of all the people disillusioned him. The sight of Donagh sitting nonchalantly on the edge of his upside-down currach convinced him. He made his way to him.

"H'm," said Donagh, "I was wonderin' if you'd turn up."

Colm didn't answer him. He just stood there and tightened his eyes against the glare of the sea. He didn't turn round where the people were crowding. What would Sorcha think of him?

"Where are the Conneelys?" he asked hopefully, hoping that they might have died in the night of convulsions.

"Here they are now," said Donagh nodding his head behind him.

They came down towards the narrow quay carrying the currach on their shoulders. Their heads were hidden under it, so that you only saw their legs walking. It looked funny. People addressed remarks to them as they arrived, and their voices and laughter boomed from inside the boat. They reached the quay and lifted the boat from their shoulders.

"Hah, so yeer here," said James. "I thought ye might have run out of the country for shame."

His brother was grinning too.

"It maight have been betther for them to have run away," he said. "Won't they be the laughin' stock of the whole of Connemara in about four hours!"

"I wouldn't waste me breath on ye," said Donagh rising. "And when Pat Kinneally gets here to start us off, I'm goin' to be sorry for the pair of ye."

"Here's oul Pat now," somebody behind said, and Pat comes down in his bowler hat, puffing, because the only exercise he ever took was pulling at porter.

"Right, min, right, min, right, min," said Pat. "Launch the crafts till we get this over. A great day," he went on, rubbing his hands and counting with his eyes the number of porter drinkers on the two necks. "We'll have a great day when this is over. This'll go down in the history of the parish, so it will, and may the best men win."

"Colm," said Sorcha, catching his sleeve and making him turn towards her.

Her hair was wild in the wind and she seemed to be angry.

"What are you doing this for?" she asked, not caring whether Donagh heard her or not. "Don't you know he only wants to make a joke of you? He doesn't care about the old race. He cares about you. He'll always say, If only I hadn't that fool of a farmer in the boat. That's what he'll say. Don't heed them now, Colm. Walk away from this with me, and if you like I'll never set a foot again in my father's house."

Colm sensed Donagh's silence; the tight anger of Sorcha. Who'd have believed it of Sorcha? Well, what am I waiting for? Nothing except the something primitive that's in all men.

"They have laughed at me before, Sorcha," he said, "and please God they'll laugh at me again. But this is different. This is something else. I'm goin' out on that sea if it's the end of me."

"It's likely to be the end of you," she said, stamping her foot. She had nice Sunday shoes on, he noticed, and her legs looked very rich in the silk stockings. "There's a good sea out there and it's a treacherous place between the two necks."

"There'll be four men in the boats," said Colm, "three fishermen and a farmer, and if I'm the only one of them that can't fish I'll take me oath I'm the only one of them that can swim and that's something."

"If you're comin'," said the voice of Donagh, "let you be launching the boat with me. If you don't want to come I'll take Sorcha."

"I'm off now, Sorcha," said Colm turning away from her.

He gave them all a big laugh then. He carefully removed his navy-blue coat and folded it and laid it on a rock. He was wearing a collar and tie and he removed these too. The two Conneelys were already in their boat on the water, holding on to the side of the pier with their thick hands. They were unshaved and had jerseys on them with the white bainin coats over them. They looked so different to the Colm on the pier in his white shirt and his trousers with the lovely crease. People around started giggling. You couldn't blame them, as men said afterwards. It was a cruel shame to have a swank like Colm getting into a currach.

They launched the boat. Colm looked out at the running sea and felt the lightness of the currach that was nothing but tarred canvas stretched over thin laths, and he didn't feel very well. All right. He tightened his jaw muscles. The currach was leaping around like a cork on the water. Donagh lowered himself into it and it steadied a bit. Colm sat in the seat behind him. The Conneelys were laying off from the pier now, riding the rough waves with seemingly effortless ease, flipping the top of the waves with the heavy oars.

Pat Kinneally was shouting, his hands around his mouth.

"Get off in a line out beyant, and let ye be ready to go on a shout."

Donagh tugged the water with his oars and they flew away from the pier. Colm tried to match his stroke with his own, but missed the wave and locked his right oar under Donagh's. The boat slewed around and headed back for the pier. He reddened at the remarks from the shore. "Let them trail," said Donagh, not sharply. "Watch my back and don't be watching me oars. When I lean, you lean; when I pull, you pull." He turned the boat again. Colm held the oars free of the waves and watched the rhythm in front of him. Then he took it up. After all he had been in boats before. It's just that this whole thing was upsetting. Rowing a currach wasn't that hard. Look at them from the shore. Nothing much to it.

They lined up beside the Conneelys, who were spitting on a hand a time as they freed them from the oars. They were grinning. Not talking, just grinning. They shouldn't have been, because Donagh was watching the shore and saw the raised hand of Pat Kinneally and saw it fall. His shout was whipped away by the wind and came late so that before they received it, cute oul Donagh was four boat lengths away and getting into his stride.

It's not too bad, Colm thought. It's a chip-chop movement. You don't dig in the oars, you chip them in and chop them out of the waves. The water was green and was breaking into white at its tops. It was also very wet. They were running parallel to the waves, so that they were up and down, up and down, and sometimes the waves broke into the boat and Colm felt the sea water on his legs, soaking through his lovely blue trousers with the tailor's crease still in them, now gone forever.

He shortly began to feel the strain on the tendons of his left arm. The waves were hitting the bow of the boat and were driving it in, and this had to be countered by stronger pulling on the left oars. It didn't matter for some time. He tightened his big hands about the oars and pulled hard. In, out, chip, chop. I could do this before my breakfast. He could see over Donagh's shoulder the Conneelys' boat coming behind them. They seemed to be pulling effortlessly. The two bodies acted as if they were on the one string. He could see muscles bulging under the clothes of Donagh's back. His neck was burned almost black from his years of sun. His neck was wrinkled and the tendons stood out on it. He's a good man in a boat, was Colm's thought. Colm tugged away joyously. They began to increase their lead.

"Take it aisy, take it aisy," he heard the voice of Donagh then. "Save a bit for the road home. Remember that."

Colm sobered. Six miles across and six miles back. That made twelve miles. Would they do three miles an hour? Say four hours. Could I keep this up for four hours? Why not? I'll show them.

They heard the people shouting behind them as they approached the other neck. They were still in the same positions. The Conneely boat was almost four boat lengths behind them, but Colm now could only see them through waves of pain.

"Pull your right now! Your right now!" he heard Donagh shouting, and he automatically put pressure on his right oar. It was almost a pleasure, because his left arm seemed to be numb. The cross waves caught them on the turn and water poured into the boat. Colm could feel it soaking into his body from the waist down. Then they were facing the crowded neck and were headed back, and the awful strain of the sea was pressing intolerably on the tendons of his right arm. He saw the people on the neck standing up waving and shouting, but he couldn't see their faces for the mist that was in front of his eyes. He thought his eyes were wanting to burst out of their sockets. He heard Donagh's voice again. "Pull with your right and bail with your left. Bail with your left, hear!" Colm let his left oar trail and fumbled behind him until his fingers found the tin can. It was rusty. He started to scoop out the water that was up as far as their shins. Donagh was doing the same, and if he could have seen, the Conneelys were doing the same. It was a relief to stretch the fingers of his hand any way than about the oar. His hands had been blistered before from the grip of a spade or a slane or a scythe or the handles of a plough, but never as painfully as this. Where blood blisters rose and burst in your palm, and when the water blister replaced the blood, you felt an intolerable agony that seemed to knife its way all over your body.

"Take it up now, take it up," said the voice of Donagh.

Colm took a pull again on his right oar.

The arms seemed to have been pulled from their sockets now and were lying loosely held there only by the skin. There was a band of something about his chest that was pressing his lungs, so that the breath came rasping from between his lips. He had to breathe often. He didn't seem able to get enough air at all. The whole world was green, enveloping him. A green world on which he rose and fell, rose and fell, and little people went with the waves who had tied ropes around all his limbs and were dragging him apart.

He heard Donagh saying strange things.

"Will we stop, Colm?" he was asking. "It wasn't a just thing to do. Let us stop now, in the name of God, and there will be shame from none for us."

Colm got some words out. "You din't call me Mister Colm," he said.

"You're a good man, Colm," he heard him say then, "and I'm an old fool."

Colm's breath was rasping from his chest.

"Donagh," he said, "can I have your daughter Sorcha?"

"Colm," said Donagh, "if I had ten daughters you could have the ten of them, but let us ease up now. It was a terrible thing I have done, and if you go on and we have to row into the shore and you a corpse, what will my daughter Sorcha say to me?"

"Donagh," said Colm, "whereabouts are your men the Conneelys?"

"They are five minutes or more ahead of us, Colm," said Donagh, "and if God above was with me in this currach now, there's not a thing even He could do about it."

"Donagh," said Colm, "let us row like fair hell and catch up the Conneelys."

He heard Donagh laughing.

"Bygod, we'll try, Colm," he said, "and, win, lose or draw, I'd fight the whole of Ireland for you and the wedding of my daughter will be the greatest event that ever happened in the province of Connacht."

The people on the shore saw a strange sight. Out there on the galloping waves, two black corks bobbing about, like corks kids throw into channels with matchsticks stuck out of them. And one was far ahead of the other and in the second boat for some time the second rower seemed to be bent double over his oars and patting at the waves as if he was playing with them, and then the man seemed to straighten and the second boat seemed to put on speed, and to be slowly and surely catching up on the boat ahead. The people from the far neck had raced across from there to this neck so that there was a great crowd on all the vantage places, and they were all stretching and leaning and crying shouts out of them like oyster catchers on lonely beaches.

Who crossed the point first? You can go back to that village now and go into Pat Kinneally's pub for a pint, and when you have become strong in drink you can express an opinion as to who won the famous currach race, and in all probability you will end up the evening with a black eye.

It was the Conneelys, I tell ye! It was not! Didn't I see with me own eyes that Donagh's boat was the width of two oar blades ahead of them? Weren't they bet to the wide, weren't they? Who ever heard the like? Two grown men against an old man and a dungboy that never saw a boat in his life and they whipped the divil out of them. Now listen, Mister Whoever you are.

Whatever happened after, that day, the four men were taken to the pier like real heroes and they were hoisted up on shoulders and carried in triumph up to Pat's place. They got four free pints, which was a record for Pat, and Colm was clapped on the back as if he was a real fisherman, and when he got out of there he headed for Sorcha's place, and she was halfway to meet him on the road. They crossed a field to where Colm had his haystack tied up for the winter and he kissed her there, and then he fainted clear away, and it took her five solid minutes of kissing him and loosening his shirt front and fanning him before he opened his eyes to the darkening sky.

He rubbed the worry from her forehead with his bruised fingers.

"I'm sorry, Sorcha," he said. "But listen, your oul fella is a great man."

"That's odd," said Sorcha who was crying, "that's the very thing he is shouting about you."

The Gauger

———◇———

H E STOPPED THE car at the byroad. He left the
engine ticking over while he wondered if he would
chance taking the car in. He got out and walked
along the road for a bit. It wasn't good. It was a dirt road deeply
rutted. He shivered in the cold January wind. The sun was shining from a steel-blue sky. The wind was coming from the mountains over in the northwest. Cold and all as it was, he could
stand awhile and admire the view. Behind him was the main
tarred road. The ground fell away from the road, fairly steeply
into a valley that held three long lakes seeming to touch one
another with the wet tips of long fingers. On this side of the
main road there was an enormous plain stretching for four
miles until it was baulked by the low mountains beyond. It
was a plain of sedge and faded heather and green prickly gorse
that was dotted with a few yellow blooms. That must be a
good plain for grouse, he thought, as he looked it over.

He decided against taking the car in. He couldn't see the
house. The road wound along until it disappeared around the
shoulder of a gorse-covered hill. He didn't think the springs
of the car could abide the bad road. So he went back to the
car, reached in, took out rubber boots, slipped out of his shoes
and put the boots on. Then he locked the car and set off.
When he was walking for a time his blood warmed and it
didn't seem to be so dreadfully cold. He was glad he hadn't
brought the car. The road was really dreadful. A mountain
stream alongside sometimes ran under it, and the bridges were
homemade and precarious. Sometimes the stream ran over the

road and had washed it away down to the sloping granite bed. He thought that this must be a lonely place to live, particularly in the winter. He knew that there was just one house in here, occupied by two brothers, Willie and Joe Mocksie. What an odd name? He tried to figure out the derivation of the name, running over Irish words in his head, but had to let it go. He judged that the house must be three miles in from the main road and was glad when he finally turned a corner and saw it up on the side of a hill settled in there snuggly with a shelter-belt of douglas and silver fir protecting it from the main blasts that must roar across the bog plain. He marvelled at how well the trees had grown in this bleak place. It was a newish house, single story, with dark blue tiles on it and two windows, one each side of the open door, looking blankly at him. There was a stable with a galvanised roof to the right of it and, outside the stable, piled manure that steamed in the cold sun.

It was quite a steep climb to the house, steps cut out of the rock by time and by cold chisel. He was puffing a bit when he stood at the open door and looked in. There was a turf fire burning in it and a man sitting with his back to the door.

He coughed and the man turned slowly to look at him. He wore a white bainin coat that was no longer white but yellow from age, and heavy homespun trousers over thick hobnailed boots. He wore a hat, shapeless and almost colourless, and his face was covered with grey stubbly whiskers that had been unevenly clipped by scissors.

"You have a nice place here," the man at the door said.

"Ah," said the old man rising and reaching for a stick by the fire. "Come in, come in and warm yourself."

"My name is Winters," the man at the door said, coming in, "Tim Winters." He wondered if his name meant anything to the old man, but it didn't, he could see that. He wondered whether to be relieved or not.

"Willie is out," the old man said. "Out on the hill. He'll be back. Willie is the talker."

"I see," said Winters, sitting on a wooden chair and warming his hands. The kitchen was very neat. There wasn't a lot in it. Just two chairs and a table and a cupboard for delf and a bag of flour in the corner, but it was a tidy kitchen.

"Nice scenery you have, too," Winters said.

"Can't eat it," said the old man sitting down again.

"True enough," Winters said, laughing.

"Have a lot of people up here, mainly in summer," the old man said. "Nothing better to do. Looking at scenery. Women in trousers. Terrible. At home having babies should be." He spat accurately into the ashes. Winters knew that he must be seventy. He didn't look it. There was only a year or two between the brothers. He knew that from the files and the searches for certificates. It always interested him to come from the cold files of people's statistics, to see the file numbers were real people of flesh and blood. Here opposite him was one half of file A/x 94763, Joseph Mocksie, approx. age 72/73, a warm-blooded old man with a healthy face and a lean bending body good for another twenty years at least.

The light was blocked out then by Willie. Winters heard his hobnail boots on the stones. He couldn't get a right look at him until he was well in. He was the image of his brother, but his face was not as hairy as Joe's and it was better clipped. His body was more bent if anything; but his eyes were not as deep-sunken, and they were more alive in his face.

"You're welcome," he said. "It isn't often we have visitors. What brings you up here?"

"I was bringing a car up here," Winters said, "and got out and decided I didn't like the look of the road, so walked it up."

"Great place, great place," Willie said. "Glad you called. Like to see visitors. Two lonely oul men. Soon be scratching holes in the ground for us. Eh, Joe?"

"Speak for yourself," Joe said, a bit sourly, with another spit.

Willie laughed.

"Joe doesn't like to think of the end," he said. "I don't mind. I've seen everything of this world I want to see. Look at me. I attended cattle on the pampas of Argentina. Would you believe that?"

"I would," said Winters looking at him.

"Aye, and you would be right," Willie said. "I have also seen America from shore to shore and I smelt the spices of China. Eh Joe? Joe was a stick-at-home, Joe was. Never saw the outside of the rim of the parish, Joe didn't."

"Where'd it get you?" Joe asked.

"Ah man!" Willie laughed, "the places it got me you wouldn't believe. I do have Joe wriggling, I tell you, with my tales. I know the feel of the skin of the women of four different breeds." He ticked them off on his fingers. "Black, brown, yellow and white. Eh, Joe?" winking at Winters.

Tim was enjoying himself, but he thought: This won't do, I'll have to get down to business.

"You seem to have a nice snug place here," he said. He thought that Joe looked at him quickly under his thick eyebrows. But Willie became expansive.

"Best little place in Connacht," said Willie. "All that whole plain out there belongs to us, and the hill here behind us. How many acres? I'll tell you. Two thousand acres."

"It's not very good land though, is it?" Winters asked.

"Good enough for us," said Willie. Joe seemed to have taken a fit of coughing. Tim was amused. He's the cute one of the two, he thought, despite all Willie's travelling. Willie paid no attention to him. "Five hundred sheep we rear out on that plain," he said. "Five hundred of the best sheep in the country and fourteen bullocks on the hills."

"With wool and beef sales, you must be very snug at that rate," said Winters.

Joe was coughing very badly.

"We do well enough," said Willie, "I know many ranchers in the Argentine that would envy us."

"At that rate," said Winters, "I don't see why you applied for the old-age pensions. With means like you have you should know that you can't qualify for the pension."

Willie was looking at him with his mouth open. Joe was cuddling his head in his hands. Tim saw the emotions on Willie's face, saw his mouth closing and his eyes narrowing.

"You're the bloody gauger!" he said, and he leaned back against the table.

"Well, officially I'm an Inspector of Old-Age Pensions," said Tim. "But unofficially I suppose I am the bloody gauger."

Willie was angry.

"You should have told us," he said. "It wasn't right not to tell us."

"I didn't get a chance to tell you," said Tim.

"You should have known goddam," said Joe. "Fella comes up in the middle of winter, what does he come for?"

"Well it was all lies," said Willie. "You know that."

"Well, no," said Tim. "I don't. Five hundred sheep and fourteen bullocks is an awful lot of capital."

"Goddam," said Joe.

"Talk," said Willie. "Nothing but talk. Where the hell would we get that many animals? What the fair hell would we do with them?"

"I don't know," said Tim.

"Come out and I'll show you," said Willie. "We'll walk it."

"The whole two thousand acres?" Tim asked.

"No two thousand acres in the bloody things," Willie said. "You look up the rating books. You'll see. Only two acres of arable and three acres of fields for hay, and the rest is all bog and scrub. Dammit, it wouldn't feed a flea. You come and see. Come on. Come on out with me and I'll show you. You'll see."

"All right," said Tim. "I'll go and look." He followed Willie out. Willie was walking fast. Tim was laughing inside as he followed him. It was a terrible catch-on. He knew the place wasn't very wealthy. He didn't know exactly how many animals they had, but he supposed they would have just enough to live. He heard Joe scuttling out of the place after them. He saw him going around the other side of the house. Willie stopped at the stable.

"Here," said Willie, going in. "That's all the animal we have, and two calves off her. Look at her, the miserable bitch!" And he gave the cow a kick in the belly. Tim wanted to laugh but he kept his face serious.

"She looks a well fed beast to me," he said. So she did. She was well taken care of as well, and Willie's kick hadn't been heavy.

"She's miserable," Willie insisted. "She'd keep you awake at night coughing. I'm sure she has T.B. It wouldn't surprise me to come out one morning and find her stone-dead, the Lord save us." He made the sign of the cross on her hip as if to make up to her for the expression.

"Well, what else now?" Tim asked.

"We'll have to go up the hill," Willie said. "Up here behind." He seemed to be making an awful hard climb of it now, and a few minutes ago he had been very active. He was puffing and blowing. Tim passed him swiftly and came over the top and was just in time to see Joe lashing furiously with his stick at two nice stumps of bullocks. He was driving them around a rock that hid the lot of them from view. Willie came up behind him, peering.

"I saw your brother driving off two nice beasts there," Tim said.

"Bad luck to them, the black bastards," Willie said, "trespassing again."

"But your nearest neighbour is eight miles away," Tim said.

"I know, the gowleog," said Willie, "but while we're asleep

at night doesn't he be driving his withered beasts on to our bit of grass."

"You should have the law on him," said Tim.

Willie showed him the two calves and then hurriedly suggested that they make their way across the plain so that he would see that it was sheepless.

Willie moved on the plain like a goat. Once they came down from the hills, the going was very soft and Tim had to walk carefully. Willie seemed to know every tussock in the place and barely wet the soles of his boots. Tim would have been wet up to the knees if he hadn't the rubber boots. They walked about half a mile in there before Tim called on him to stop.

"We've gone far enough here now," he said. "I can see all I want to see from here."

"It's little you'll see, I swear to you," said Willie.

Tim swung around. He could see the little round patches on the hills away and an occasional one out on the plain, as if somebody had scattered white balls of wool. He started slowly to count them, pointing his finger at each one.

"I make out," he said, "that there are fifty-nine sheep grazing your land."

He kept his face serious.

Willie was looking at him. His face was suffused. Tim thought for a moment that he would use the stick on him.

"You should have told us you were the gauger," Willie said.

Then he turned back, taking a slightly oblique way towards the hills. Tim followed after him. In a minute, he thought, I will tell him that that many sheep and even the two hidden bullocks do not disqualify him from the pension; but let him stew awhile. It'll teach him to stop telling tall stories. Then he had to concentrate on where he was walking because the ground seemed to have become very soft. Every inch of it seemed to be nothing but quaking bog. He had to be careful of every step and walk only where the butts of the round rushes showed. Finally he had to stop because there seemed to be no way ahead that was not soft. He raised his head. Willie seemed suddenly to be a long way ahead of him. He was leaping like a hare, the bent body jumping and twisting. Tim called after him.

"Hey, Willie, how do I get out of here?" To his surprise Willie didn't turn his head. I didn't notice that he was deaf, Tim thought. He called again. "Hey, Willie! Willie!" Willie didn't turn his head. The effort of calling had made him lose his balance. One foot went ahead of him; the weight of his body came on it, and almost before he knew it he was up to his hips in brown muck. It was very cold. He turned back and grabbed at the rushes where he had been standing. He pulled hard at them. Part of them came away in his hand and he fell back again. He caught the remainder and pulled hard, and gradually hauled himself from the mire. He had to leave his rubber boot behind him. He crouched there on the little quaking tussock and the sweat broke out on him. What's this? he thought. He didn't mean to do this deliberately, surely? Still holding, he turned his head and called after the figure that was small now, it was so far away. "Hey! Hey! Willie! Willie!" he called. But he might as well have been calling the moon.

"I'll have to go back the way I came," he said out loud. Then he looked and he couldn't seem to see what way he had come. All around, the ground appeared to be green and slimy. He panicked for a few seconds. But nobody would kill another person, he thought, over a lousy pension of a few shillings a week. He thought he saw tracks. He couldn't stay here all night. Because night would soon be here. The sun was gone behind the hills. The sky around was the colour of orange peel. Without the sun the wind blew very cold.

He stepped off the tussock. He went to his hips. He threw himself forward. He felt his face wet. He was in the muck up to his hips again. Suppose the rest of me goes? He pulled out his leg that was free of the boot and kicked and hauled until his other leg came, leaving the boot behind it. His body was on top of the bog, half sunken in the mire. He edged along it like a frog using his legs, and his arms flailing. When he thought he was making no progress, he felt the butt of rushes under one hand and he hauled himself on to it. He paused there. He tried to calm himself. He said: This couldn't happen to me. Then he took off his overcoat. It was a heavy wool coat. He spread it on the bog in front of him, walked across it and before it sank under his weight he had found another hard tussock. He gripped this, retrieved his coat and went on again.

Joe was making the tea when Willie came in. Joe looked at him.

"Big mouth," said Joe. "Goddam big mouth."

"And he saw you chasing off the two beasts," said Willie.

"That's that," said Joe. "Is he gone home now?"

"I don't know," said Willie, "I don't know where the bastard is gone. I left him out there."

Joe looked at him sharply.

"Out there where?" he asked. He didn't like the look in Willie's eyes. "He's nowhere near the Swallow?" he asked. "Well, is he?"

Willie was sour. "He was crossing it when I left him," said Willie.

It was very quick the way Joe hit him across the face with the thin end of the stick. "You, you," he said. "Talk, talk, talk. Travel, travel, travel! What good? Tell me what good?" Then he was out the door and away.

Tim was on the point of giving up. He was lying across his overcoat doing as the frogs do with hands and legs. But it was very severe going. He thought: Who'd ever think that a fellow could die like this over a goddam lousy pension? What harm, but I liked the two old birds. I liked them.

Then he heard the calling. It was dusk now. You could distinguish nothing unless you saw it against the sky. First he thought it might be the call of a grouse or a snipe. He struggled on a bit. Then he listened. He heard it again. It was a man calling. He called back, "Here! Here!" hoping that a grouse wouldn't call, "Go-back! Go-back! Go-back!" like they do. He kept calling. He didn't feel he had enough energy to do anything else. Just to keep calling while his tired and wet and muddy body sank the coat lower in the bog.

Then he felt it quaking under him and he saw the figure and the stock being held out to him. He caught it. He would never let it go. He pulled himself after it and then Joe (it would have to be Joe, the other one would never come back) was steadying him. "Follow me," said Joe. "Where I put a foot you put a foot!" Tim followed him, and in five minutes Joe said: "It's all right now. We're on good ground."

"My coat is back there," said Tim.

"Better your coat than you," said Joe. "Come up to the house. Dry off."

"No," said Tim. "He's an old man. Even so I would have to hit him. I haven't ever hit an old man."

"Forgive him," said Joe. "It's the travel. All that travel. It upsets them."

"That's right," said Tim, "travel is dangerous."

"Forget pensions," said Joe. "Very sorry, man, very sorry."

"I'm the sorry one," said Tim. "That's the terrible part of it. You'll get the pension. That's the trouble. I'm not bad enough. See, Joe. That's my trouble. Maybe I haven't travelled enough."

"You're a good man," said Joe.

Tim laughed. It was a still night. He heard his laugh hitting off the hills and coming back to him.

The Young Turk

———◇———

CECIL WAS WALKING down by the Docks. It was September and he was thinking that in only a few more days he would be going back to the boarding school. The prospect didn't please him. He was a neat boy. He wore a navy blue worsted suit, neatly pressed, and a cream-coloured shirt and a red-and-black tie, which were the colours of his school. The cap he wore was red, and it bore the school crest on the front of it, just over the peak. His skin was very clear and clean and lightly tanned. He looked well. His eyes were brown and were rather wide and innocent-looking.

It was a warm day. The sun was hidden behind misty clouds. There was little wind. It was a day that would induce torpor in an ant. He stood and watched the men unloading the coal boat. The winches were creaking, lazily it seemed. The shouts of the donkey engine man were lazy. Even the coal falling from the chutes into the carts seemed to fall lazily. Farther ahead a bigger crane was hoisting large baulks of timber from the bowels of a ship as if they were bunches of matches.

Cecil decided to cross the road and walk by the ships.

He had barely put his foot on the road when a bicycle came around the corner of the nearest byroad and swerved to avoid him. There was a boy on the bicycle. It was a heavy bicycle with a small front wheel to accommodate a large frame for holding a big basket.

The boy called him a nasty name. Cecil let the name go over his head.

"I beg your pardon," he said in his neat cultivated voice.

The other had stopped the bicycle, one foot on the ground. He was frowning furiously. He was considering further action. Then he looked closely at Cecil and his eyebrows rose.

"Why, Prissy," he said then, "what are you doing down here?"

Cecil was really pleased to see him.

"Turk," he said, and went close to him. Fifteen-year-old boys didn't shake hands like adults but he put his hand on the handlebars of the bicycle close to Turk's hand and looked at him with warm eyes. They were of a height, but Turk was more solidly built. He still wore his spiky hair very closely cut so that he looked like an old-time convict. The eyes were small and narrow, the nose pug, and the face broad. His clothes were clean; but they were well patched and darned, and the shoes on his feet were the same. There were no creases in Turk's trousers.

"I'm just down for a walk," said Cecil. "Going back to school next week."

"Very posh," said Turk, aping his speech. "Jolly old school and what not. Bit different from the old National, eh, Prissy?"

Cecil thought of the old National school he had attended with Turk, and he tried to see it in comparison with the expensive boarding school where he was now. He laughed.

"It's different all right, Turk," he said.

"I'll bet," said Turk rubbing his nose in the old habit he had. It was just a rub forward and back and a slap of the thumb. Cecil used to say to him about it that in twenty years he would have his nose worn away.

"What are you doing?" Cecil asked.

"What do you think?" Turk asked, giving the bicycle a vicious kick. "What do you expect? Just working. Delivering messages. Did you think I should be going to college or what?"

"Well," said Cecil. He thought back to the old school. They called Turk the Young Turk, because he was a bit of a handful. Cecil had been sent to this National school because, as his father told everyone, they were democrats and they liked their son to mix with the "local boys." If he had kept quiet about it it wouldn't have sounded like the dreadful small-town snobbery that it was. Cecil had a tough time at school. He spoke well because that was the way his mother insisted on him speaking and he looked a bit delicate and girlish, and besides he had that dreadful name. He was about a year establishing himself. All in all he must have lost about a half-pint of blood before he became used to being called Prissy. His last big fight had been with Turk, whose real name was Paddy. Turk beat him of course. Turk could beat anybody. He was strong and vicious and always remained very cold when he was fighting. But they got to like each other in the middle of the fighting. For the last two years at school Cecil had as much trouble at home about being seen around with Turk as Turk had had all his life – because trouble and he appeared to be sleeping companions.

It all seemed a long time ago now. They were practically grown up. Turk working! Imagine that! Cecil thought that Turk would do better at college than he ever would, because he had more brains than any of the good boys. That was life, Cecil thought. Some people were poor, and some people weren't poor.

"Do you know, Turk," he said, "I haven't really had any fun since we left the National. Everyone is shocking respectable. We had good times, didn't we, those times."

Turk was pleased.

"We had," he said. "Do you remember the night we went playing ghosts up in the old graveyard?"

Cecil shivered. "I won't ever forget that," he said.

"And the time we whipped the schoolmaster's trousers," said Turk.

47

Cecil laughed.

There were many other things. They were always slightly dangerous. It seemed to Cecil that all of them ended up with the Turk being beaten and accepting the beating stoically.

"Where you going now?" Turk asked.

"Just wandering around the docks," said Cecil.

"I'll go down with you," said Turk.

"Shouldn't you be working?" Cecil asked.

"Ach, that," said Turk. "Hump them. They tell you to be back in half an hour. They don't expect you for an hour. I can get another job. I'll go down a bit with you."

They walked on, talking about long ago and oddly enough recapturing some of the pleasure and the danger, and Cecil thought what a pity it was that his whole life henceforward would be cut away from the life of Turk, on account of the accident of one's father being born poor and the other well salted. It was puzzling, but it was part of life. He tried to place Turk in the school where he himself was now. He didn't fit in. Academically yes, but otherwise he wouldn't last twenty-four hours. They walked to where the long pier stretched out into the sea. They sat on it with their legs dangling. It was a long way down to the water, which was indolently lapping against the great baulks of wood bolted to the concrete. There were imbedded steel ladders reaching down to the sailing vessels moored below.

Cecil saw Turk looking closely at one of them. It was a neat dinghy and it was called Mary. It was obviously the possession of a proud owner. It was beautifully scrubbed and well painted and protected. A neat city seaman, Cecil thought, and then Turk said, "Come on, let's go fishing," and turned his body and set off down the ladder towards that very boat.

"Look here," said Cecil. He was law-abiding. He always counted the cost. Turk was halfway down looking up at him.

"What's wrong with you?" he asked.

"Won't you lose your job?" Cecil asked feebly.

"Oh, that's gone long ago," said Turk.

Cecil knew he shouldn't. His father was a frightfully law-abiding man too. But there you are. He was already halfway down the ladder. Turk hoisted the sail (it was beautifully and methodically gathered and tied) while Cecil threw off the bow and stern ropes, and his qualms along with them; untied the port oar and pushed the little boat away from the wall. The sail rose out of its almost mathematically correct creases and the little boat sailed out into the bay. They looked at each other and grinned. This was more like it; better than the pallid and boring boarding-school days; delivering to Mrs Murphy her rashers and sausages and strawberry jam. It was such a neat little boat with its varnish glittering even in the dull sunshine. The boards were hot to the touch. There was a nice little breeze on the bay. It just bellied the sail. But that was all the boat wanted. She was so light and airy that you could nearly sail her blowing your breath at her.

"Nice boat," said Turk, asking for praise as if she were his own. He certainly knew where everything was. He burst the screws from the lock with a pull of his fingers. The little cupboard under the seat was exposed. Cecil didn't like seeing the raped lock on the door. It seemed to spoil the symmetry which the owner had lavished on his boat with almost fanatical correctness. Turk took two fishing frames from the shelf in there and threw one up to Cecil. He caught it. Brown line wound around precisely, with a heavy lead weight on it and ending in a red spinner. He was building up a picture of the owner of a boat. A small natty little man anyhow, precise, who would love his boat maybe more than he loved the sea. He wouldn't be a professional who would curse the sea and yet be tied to it like a drunkard to a troll.

He loosed the line from the frame, dropped the heavy weight off and unwound it. It was hardly unwound when he was pulling it in again from the tug of a mackerel, flashing silver in the sunlight. He whooped, and so did Turk. They were passing through a shoal and soon the lovely varnish was potted and pitted with the scales and blood of the rigidly threshing fish. Six times they passed over shoals, until they were well out into the bay, and the catching of them was turning into monotony. It was then of course that Cecil looked around him and was afraid. Because the sea wasn't calm. The haze over the sun had darkened to a dirty bronze colour and the wind was driving in gusts that scalped the top of the waves and scooped them away with a howl. The little boat suddenly appeared to be very small. He wound in his line. Turk had his in already and was leaning on the tiller. He had to get the boat around. He had to do it in a very wide sweep, and each time a gust came, four in all, before she was headed into the wind, so that the little boat was half full of water and the dead fish were floating in it and grinning maliciously. Cecil prayed and tried to scoop the water out with his cupped hands. He was kneeling in it so it was easy to pray. He thought: What will the poor little precise man think of his lovely boat? And he thought: I should have known; things always happen like this with Turk.

Turk was shouting at him, but the wind was stealing his words. Then the wind stole the sail. It happened just like that. Whip, flap, whip, and the sail was gone away and the boat was floundering in a dip with the waves looming eight feet above it. They weren't coloured a gentle grey-green any longer. They were all dull grey with the tops of them white. Can things happen so quickly? Certainly. Look how quick you can steal a nice little boat and wreck it. Cecil was wet to the skin. Turk had left the tiller and was unlashing the oars. They fitted into the irons, but they were not fixed rowlocks. He sat and tried to pull the head of the boat into the wind. It was a very stiff job. He couldn't quite do it. He held it sideways, and the waves hit it a few left jabs and doused it and flowed on top of it and Cecil kept scooping, scooping. And he thought: It is nice that the boat is being washed from the blood and the scales. And then Turk couldn't hold one of the oars. It lifted out of the iron and it went away on a wave, and before it went it flicked Cecil on the head passing by. He felt the clout. It knocked him flat on his face in the water. He swallowed some of it as he gasped. It tasted terrible of salt and fish and blood and varnish and bits of other things. Then he emerged. Turk was trying to hold the boat with the other oar held over the stern, trying to scull her around. Cecil felt very woozy in the head. He shook it again and again. He flicked blood away from it each time. He was squatting, his knees and palms on the floorboards. He saw Turk with his mouth open shouting, and then the whole lot of them boat and all were wiped out as if they had never been. He felt the wood leaving him and he held his breath. He didn't think: This is the end of one boy at a boarding school and of a messenger boy in a shop. The blow kept him from thinking. He would undoubtedly have died if Turk's groping hands hadn't found him and gripped on to his hair. He felt that – as if his scalp was rising off his skull; and then he felt himself being banged on the ribs as if he was being kicked by a draughthorse. Then his face was free and he was breathing and he was kicked a few more times. He felt the slippery seaweed rocks under his hands, and he sensed himself hauled and hauled and turned over on his back. His eyes were shut. He was afraid to open them until he became confident. That was Turk calling all right. "Hey, Cecil! Cecil! Hey, wake up, can't you!" He never called me Cecil before, he thought. It was always Prissy. That's what he said, when he opened his eyes. "Here, Turk, you shouldn't call me Cecil."

He saw Turk's face. It was bloody. There was a deep cut over his eye. But it was a strong face filled with anxiety.

"I'm sorry, Prissy," said Turk. "Honest I'm sorry."

"Don't, for God's sake," said Cecil. He sat up. They saw the two men in oilskins running towards them across the rough shore. They had been thrown up on the island of the lighthouse. He saw that now. The sky was very dark and the light in the white house was flashing yellow.

The men lifted them to their feet. "Ye goddam fools!" one man said. "Have ye no more sense than to go out in a bloody boat with the storm signals flying in the harbour?"

The poor boat, thought Cecil, and looked around for it. It wasn't to be seen. It might never have existed. It could have been a phantasy. The men shouted some more at them. Cecil waited for the stubborn look to come on Turk's face. It came.

It never left his face until they finally parted. Cecil always remembered it. With that on his face how could Cecil say: I don't care, Turk. I enjoyed it, the sin and the punishment. How could he say: By the way, Turk, thanks for saving my life.

They were four hours drying off inside there and getting their wounds iodinized, sitting in clothes too big for them until their own were dried over the roaring stove. And then they crossed the few hundred yards to the harbour in the calm sea watching the people on the pier coming closer and closer. Yes, his father was there, tall and stern, and his mother, pale and worried, and behind was the big car belonging to his father, waiting fat and fulsome to absorb him. There were other people waiting and watching too. Cecil dropped his eyes. Turk was looking at the pier with his mouth a thin line and his eyebrows closing down on his eyes.

They climbed the ladder. Oh, Cecil! Cecil! His mother. She smelled very nice; her skin was soft. There were tears left on his cheek from her. His father: ashamed that they were the centre of an exhibition. Hustling to the car. But a look back over his shoulder and he saw two things hard to forget. The big blue-jerseyed fisherman who was Turk's father raising a fist and hitting Turk on the side of the head. Not a hard blow. Hard enough to stagger him. It was a blow of exasperation, a blow of shame that a man was made a public spectacle by his son. And there was an enormous fat man with small hands. He had a long brown beard and little hair on his head and he was dancing from foot to foot and he was crying: "But the boat? The boat? What has happened to my beautiful boat?" And then Cecil was in the car and they were going home in silence. And he thought: What is the use of telling them that Turk saved my life when they would say he endangered it in the beginning? There was no good word for Turk. Just in his own mind forever there would be. He would have to wait until he was a man, until he could walk and talk with Turk again. But that was a time away, and would Turk be the same then? Would he be the same then? And that's why Cecil cried at that point.

The Proud Man

———◦———

GAEGLERS AND TOM BULGER were sitting at a table in a small country pub with two pints of beer in front of them when the man came in the door dragging his leg behind him. At least, it looked like that. It was just that the leg was a bit crooked, and he had a job bringing it up. He was tall and lean, with a fine column of a neck and powerful shoulders, and he wore a greying moustache and shabby but very clean clothes. He was about fifty, Gaeglers thought.

Gaeglers and Tom had been friends since the time Tom led him on a vain hunt for wild geese as a just atonement for a deceit Gaeglers had practised on Tom's brother, who owned a shop in the small Irish seacoast town Gaeglers came from. Gaeglers' way of earning a living was precarious but profitable, and consisted mainly of making money without working for it. It involved a little homespun philosophy, a touch of psychology, a lack of conscience, a lot of confidence, the ability to class people as possibles and probables, squealers or non-squealers, and a very delicate sense of what was legal and illegal. Gaeglers always gave his profession as "factor." He liked Tom. He forgave him for the wetting he got on the wild-goose chase (he fell in a boghole), and now if things became a little hot in the town he would mount a bus, ride the few miles to the village in the mountains where Tom lived, and stay there until everything was cool again. Tom and his wife were always pleased to see him. He livened things up for them. Also, he could be quite useful, because he was strong and not unwilling to work hard when there was no possibility of his making any money out of it.

Tom addressed the man with the crooked leg with what Gaeglers thought was unusual friendliness. "And how are you, Bartley?" he asked.

The man looked at Tom, took his hand out of his pocket, where it was fumbling for coins, and came over. He shook hands. "Good evening, Tom," he said, "It was a great harvest, thanks be to God."

"It was, too," said Tom, and then he introduced the man to Gaeglers.

Gaeglers felt two pale-blue eyes looking him over. They were quiet and rather kindly eyes.

"How do you do, sir?" said Bartley, shaking his hand. His handclasp was very firm and dry.

Gaeglers still wasn't used to older people in the country calling him "sir". Later on, he realised that the "sir" was a reflex, used merely because he was dressed as a townsman. What they really thought about you emerged only after a time. If they took to laying extreme emphasis on the "sir", you could be sure that you had been judged and found wanting.

Tom and Bartley talked some about the weather, and then Bartley went back and ordered a pint and paid for it carefully and didn't look one way or the other but drank it and went out.

This wasn't right, Gaeglers knew. There was something amiss here, when a man didn't say, "What are you drinking?" or wasn't deeply insulted if you refused to drink with him. "What's wrong?" he asked Tom. "Who is he?"

Tom sighed. "He's a proud man," he said.

Apparently being proud was a very serious thing, Gaeglers thought. It seemed to be the same as being dead. "Well, I'm a proud man," said Gaeglers. "There's nobody in the whole country has more pride than me, and I'm not downhearted about it."

"It's not that," said Tom. "Long ago – Why, even when I was

a kid, I remember Bartley. There used to be great sports and galas and things around here years and years ago, when there was a lot of people and the young ones usen't to emigrate when they were hardly out of the shell. Bartley was a powerful man, I remember. It was a sight to see him stripped. Everything he'd win, I tell you – throwing the stone and vaulting the pole and running three mile and swimming in the lake. He was like a trout. Or riding the bicycle – you had to work hard at bicycles in them days to move them, I can tell you. He was a great man."

"What happened to his leg?" Gaeglers asked. "A very simple thing," said Tom. "He was building a wall and a big rock fell on his leg. It was broke in several places. He wouldn't go to a doctor. There was an oul bonesetter up the road. He went to him. It never set proper. It always had a drag in it like you see."

"And is he down on his luck now, or what?"

"He's down," said Tom. "And he'll soon be out. He had a few childer. They went away. Not doing very well. Just keeping themselves going. He has one girl at home with him. She's not young, either. Didn't marry. He can't work as hard as he used to, so the place is going to go one of these days. He's back on the taxes, and that's that."

"But why can't you all chip in?" Gaeglers asked. "Why can't we have a collection or do something like that?"

"Isn't that what I'm telling you, man!" Tom exclaimed. "He's a proud man. There's not a sinner in the place would dare go near him with money in their fist. He's a quiet sort of man, but if somebody did that he'd eat them. They'd never get away alive from him."

"Oh," said Gaeglers, thinking it over. "Then I'm not a proud man. I find it hard to believe that there are actually people like that."

"Well, there are, and he's the flower of them," said Tom. "And the trouble is that he is very well wished for here and nobody has a bad word in their mouth for him, which is a very unusual thing, I can tell you, and there's nobody that wouldn't do anything at all to save him, if he wasn't so goddam proud. When they are like that, there is no way out."

"I see," said Gaeglers. "I see." And Tom, who knew him fairly well by now, looked at him suspiciously.

It was about a week later that Gaeglers and Tom called at Bartley's house one afternoon. Bartley was mending a harness, and his daughter was churning. They put their tasks aside to welcome the two callers and wiped off a couple of chairs and set the kettle to boil. There was no use protesting about it. They talked about the weather and the price of pigs, which was remarkably high, and Bartley said it was a pity he hadn't a few of them but it cost so much to buy even a sucking bonham, and after a while the visitors came around to the object of their call.

"We need your help," said Gaeglers.

Bartley looked him straight between the eyes, but Gaeglers was ready for him. He looked bland and innocent, so Bartley believed him. "Well, now," he said, and he was pleased. "Anything at all I can do for ye and I will be only too pleased."

"It's this way," said Gaeglers. "Even in the town where I come from, we have heard some strange tale about the great men that is produced out here, leapers and swimmers and rock throwers, and we were all in there in the pub the other night and they were spinning the tales about how wonderful ye all were, and to tell you the truth, if I was to believe a half of it, the boasting that went on – Finn mac Cumhail was only trotting after the lot of you – and I said, well, if ye are as good as ye are supposed to be, let's have a sports and see what ye are like."

"And then I said," said Tom, "that young and all as they were there wasn't a one of them could hold a candle to you, Bartley; that if one of your feet was stuffed in your mouth and your two hands were tied behind your back you could leave the whole of the young fellows standing – powerful and all as they thought themselves."

Gaeglers nodded. " So I said let's go over and ask Bartley to take on the whole bloody lot of you, fair and square, bicycle, stone, and swim, and they can hammer out the other events amongst themselves," he said. "And also," he added, licking his lips, "we will have a competition for all the young girls of the place to see who is the most beautiful."

There had been long meetings at the pub about how much money Bartley would need and how much he could win in the three events without his suspicions being aroused. In order to spread the prize money a bit, Gaeglers had thought of the beauty competition. "Bartley has a daughter," he had said. "Well, that's that. The four events will be sufficient, and Bartley will have a new start." "Have you ever seen Bartley's daughter?" one of the young fellows had asked. "I don't care if she has a cork leg and can see around corners," Gaeglers had replied. "As long as she can stand and wear a blouse, she can win a beauty competition."

Now he was conscious of Bartley's daughter behind him. Well, she has nice brown hair, anyhow, he was thinking. She was a big girl, and her teeth were all right, even if they were a bit large, and she had a kindly smile, like her father. The rest of her wasn't so good, but she was a nice girl; Gaeglers knew that. He was an expert at knowing what people were like from a first look, because his living depended on it.

"So," he went on hurriedly, "since you are the father of athletics in the area, we would be very honoured if you would enter for the events, and if you would do us this honour of pitting yourself against these young boasters, they would have to pay a fee to try and best you, and the prizes for the winner would be good and substantial – cash prizes, because we have no time to be going buying medals and cups and china and things."

"No," said Bartley. Tom and Gaeglers held their breaths. "It's very kind of you, but I couldn't do it. I would wish to pay an entrance fee for the events like everyone else."

Gaeglers let his breath go slowly. "Well, all right," he said grudgingly. "I'm willing to take your shilling to cover the three events."

"Is that all?" Bartley asked.

"That's right," said Gaeglers. "There's so many entered that the fee can be reduced an awful lot." Now, he was thinking, we'll have to get every able- and disabled-bodied man in the place to enter to make up the difference between the fees and the prize money. "And if your daughter would like to enter the other competition, we will take sixpence from her, too."

He turned and looked at her directly. He didn't like the clear way she looked back at him. There was a slight smile on her lips. She is too shrewd, that one, he was thinking. I'll bet she won't.

"Of course she will, of course!" said Bartley, going over to her and putting a hand on her shoulder. "And I'd back her to the hilt. There isn't a better or more beautiful girl in the whole parish than Julia."

The other three were startled. He meant it. Julia looked at Gaeglers almost inquiringly. To hell with it, she knows, he thought. He nodded.

"All right," said Julia. "Thanks, Father, but maybe you are a bit blind."

"No, girl," said Bartley, "I'm not blind. You are a good girl. I wouldn't give a tip of your finger for all the women in the world."

"Gaeglers, here, will be the judge of everything," said Tom. "He's had experience of things like this, and since he is a stranger amongst us, he won't be backing any horse, so everything will be fair and even and aboveboard." And he added, under his breath, "God forgive me for the lies."

Bartley's eyes were shining. "Man, but it'll be a great day," he said. "It's made me feel young again, do ye know that? The oul leg'll be a bit of a handicap, but wait'll ye see, wait'll ye see!"

"That's the stuff," said Gaeglers. "We'll hold it on Sunday next, after last Mass. It'll be the biggest day in history." Then he and Tom were outside and rubbing the sweat off their foreheads. "I never had to work so hard in all me life just to give money away," said Gaeglers. "God preserve us from proud men."

The day of the sports the sun shone brightly. The field, which belonged to Bartley, was very gay with bunting, and bicycles glinting in the light, and there were a few stalls selling fruit and soft drinks and souvenirs. These were operated by Gaeglers' friends from the town, and they were naturally willing to pay him a little commission for arranging the event and informing them in time about it, so they could get onto the field first. Gaeglers explained to Tom that although he was doing all these things for love of humanity and Bartley, still he had to live, and his share of the stalls was legitimate business. Tom understood this and remarked cheerfully that Gaeglers would make money out of his mother's funeral.

All the young men were threatened in advance by Gaeglers. They could try to win in the other events, but the man who beat Bartley in the stone, the bike, or the lake would be in for a poor time, he said. They all swore their solemn oaths, but Gaeglers had doubt, because they were all healthy and excitable young men and might forget their oaths in the heat of the contests.

They did. They tried hard to win, feeling it would be shameful to be bested by an old man. But Bartley was in great condition, apart from his leg, and when he stripped off his shirt and held the heavy stone at shoulder height, you could see the muscles under his pale skin leaping and bunching, and when he had the last throw and did a half-circle and the stone left his hand, Gaeglers was horrified to see the distance it went. There was a resounding cheer all over the place. Bartley said that it was just practice – that he had flung the stone so often it was second nature to him.

It's hard to ride a bike on grass. Gaeglers put Bartley about two hundred yards ahead of the field. Bartley politely wheeled his bike back again to the starting line. Everyone was grinning. Gaeglers set them off, cursing. It was a two-mile ride, ten times around the big uneven field. Bartley fell behind and then started catching up. There was no trick in it. Then he and a powerful young man were out ahead of the others, but the young man would have got ahead of him and finished first if somebody hadn't flung a small rock accurately at the front wheel of his bicycle and brought him down, bruised and cursing and ready for murder. Gaeglers denied that he had flung the rock.

So, two up for Bartley. When it was time for the lake event, all the ladies had to be kept away, because there were the most peculiar kinds of bathing costumes among the contestants. Bartley went into the water in his long woollen winter drawers, and some of the young fellows went in with old trousers tied by a bit of twine, which fell off and left them swimming in their birthday suits, and at the end there was great laughing and chortling when they came ashore. Bartley won, but he won fair and square. He had a powerful way of lying over the water and using his two great arms to pull him along. Nobody could touch him.

Gaeglers was very pleased. There were three money prizes ready to be handed over to Bartley. Now all Gaeglers had to do was give Julia the prize for being the best beauty, and there you were. The girls were gathered on a mound in the middle of the field. Gaeglers became suddenly upset when he saw them closely. There were six of them besides Julia. The six girls were painfully pretty. That was the trouble — they were really pretty, and one of them was even beautiful. They had slim waists and fine hair, and they were very well dressed. Julia looked good in a summer dress, all right, anybody could see that, but anybody who would award her the prize over the six other girls would have to go and get his eyes examined. Gaeglers was upset for another reason, too. He had meant to talk to the six girls beforehand, as he had done with the young men, and explain to them why they wouldn't be winning any first prizes, but in the rush, and on account of having so much to attend to, he had completely forgotten to warn them, and wouldn't there be a riot among them now if he proceeded with the set plan? He cursed his forgetfulness. Then he hardened himself, and after making a little speech to the girls he was prepared to do his job, until he saw the eyes of Julia beseeching him. She knew, all right. She had come as far as this for the sake of her father, but to go on would be a terrible thing to inflict on her. Gaeglers saw that. And because he was soft over some things, what did he do but award the prize to the real beauty, and all he got for it was a kiss on the side of the neck from the winner and thanks from the eyes of Julia.

Also, the event cost him money. The prize money was short by the losing of the beauty competition, so Gaeglers had to go up to Bartley and say, "You're a great man, Bartley, there's no mistake, and if I wore a hat I'd take it off to you, and do you see those fellows in the stalls? Well, since this is your field they are paying a small rent for the use of it, and so you have this much more coming to you." And he had to hand over his percentage from the stalls.

Presently, Julia took him aside and said, "Goodbye, Gaeglers. I am very grateful for what you have done. I won't forget ever what you have done for us."

"Don't be so daft!" Gaeglers said. "All bloody women are

daft! Why have women to be so goddam daft?" He was mad, and his neck was red, but Julia smiled after him as he went furiously away.

"I set out to do a good deed," he exclaimed to Tom on the way back to Tom's house, "and what happens? I get jilted out of money. I'm never going to come out here again to you, that's sure. Every time I come out here to you, something sinister happens to me."

"Your trouble, Gaeglers, is that you're a good crook," Tom said, and he slapped his thigh and laughed like hell.

The Green Hills

———◇———

"WHAT'S THE USE of cryin'?" he asked.

"It makes your eyes sparkle," she said.

"It also makes them red and ugly," he said.

"Well, at least," she said, "they are my own eyes and I can do what I like with them."

They were silent for a time.

They sat beneath the brow of the green hill. They could see the village below them and the silent sea out beyond as placid as a good dream. The red sun was just about to plunge into the sea. You'd almost listen to hear the sizzling sound it should make. That was on their right. And on their left the moon was in the sky, crescented, its light lit, ready with its feeble but fertile challenge to the departing sun. It was a warm evening. The bracken on which they sat was crinkly dry.

He was leaning back on his elbow, plucking at the fading blossoms of the heather, idly, tearing it with strong brown fingers.

"The village looks nice now from here," he said.

It did. It was small. There were six houses, all newly built inside the last few years. Some of them were plastered with a white cement, some of them roughcast with a cream dash. They sat in a regular half-circle around the small quay. The school was in the middle. The priest came over from the other side to say Mass there on Sundays. It looked nice. You could see four currachs drawn up on the yellow sands and the mast of a hooker, rope-festooned, rising from the far side of the quay. There was a dog barking in the street. They were high up on the hill. Over from them around the shoulder of the hill, a mountain stream rushed down to seek the sea. It didn't rush much now. It wanted rain to make it roar. But you could hear it if you listened for it.

"It looks nice," she said. "I hope you will remember it."

"I know it's nice," he said. "I will probably remember it. But there are bound to be places just as nice as it."

"Do you mean that, now," she asked, "or are you only saying it because you're beginning to feel lonely already?"

Her back was towards him, her head bent. It was a good back, a good strong back, tapering to a narrow waist. Her hair, cut short for utility sake, was brown with flecks of lighter hair bleached by the sun. He knew her face. It was broad and handsome, well shaped and firm. That was it – firm. Firm eyebrows and a small firm nose and chin with the lips turned out as if they were pursed. Her eyes were startlingly light blue and direct, but they could be soft.

"No," he said, "I'm not getting lonely already. I have been away before."

"But this time you won't be coming back," she said.

"I don't know," he said. "I might, but I hope I won't be coming back. I hope that if I come back I will come back with money in my pocket which I will spend freely and that I will go away again, and that this time you will come with me."

"No," she said.

"Why, but why?" he asked.

"We've said it all before," she said. "What's the use, Derry?"

"What the hell is there below there?" he asked with an impatient sweep of his arm, "that binds you to it?"

"I just like it, that's all," she said. "That's all. I just like it. I like what we have and I don't think anywhere else could be the same as it, and I just like it, that's all."

"How can you know?" he asked. "How in the name of God can you know until you see other places to compare with it?

Are you happy to spend your whole life here, growing old and dying and never to have been out of it?"

"I am," she said.

"Well, I'm not," he said decisively. "You talk about the green hills. What green hills? You talk about green hills as if there weren't any green hills anywhere else in the world. There are. I saw them. I saw green hills that'd make this one look like it had the mange." He got up and then stooped and took her hand and pulled her up to face him. He was tall; he looked down at her face. She looked at him. "Didn't I tell you you'd make your eyes red? They are. Listen, Martha, there's just this difference between us. You want to stay here. I want to go away from it. That's the only difference. One of us will have to give way. We know what it means. What it will mean not to be together. I tell you when I come back for you you will forget the green hills."

"There's more between us," she said, looking into the restless eyes. "You have shocking ambition. That's between us. Why can't you be ambitious here? Why do you have to go three thousand miles to be ambitious?"

"Here! What's here?" he asked breaking away from her. "Nothing. Work, work, work. What you get. You get enough to eat. New suit in a year, a bicycle on the hire purchase. Cycle ten miles to a picture. Six miles to a dance. Year in year out. Gloom in the winter. Fish, shoot. But we're not getting anywhere. We're not just doing anything. I just can't stand it. You know what can happen. I'll get on. I'll get on fast. I have it up here. I'll become somebody. You'll see."

"That's the trouble," she said. "I know you will, and I don't know that you'll be the better of it." The broad shoulders, the close-cropped hair, the brown strong face and the restless eyes. Oh, he'd get somewhere all right. He was like a big city man at this moment with his well cut double-breasted suit and the white shirt and light shoes looking incongruous on the

67

side of a Connemara hill. He came back to her. He put his big arms around her. She could feel his breath on her face.

"You'll change, my girl," he said. I could change in a minute, she thought, when I am as close to him as this. "You can't whip our feeling. You'll see. I'm willing to put up with it until I come back for you. I'll make that gift to you, the fact that I have to come back to you, that I can't force you to come with me. You wait for me. You take up with any of the lads below and I'll murder them, you'll see. You hear that."

"I do," she said. They heard his father's voice calling then. He was coming up the hill. He kissed her hard. Her lips were bruised against her teeth. But she strained to him. Almost his heart missed a beat, at the thought that he would be without her. But the restlessness came back to him. A four-engined plane winging over the sea with a gigantic continent below waiting to be conquered by Derry O Flynn. It would be done. Lesser men had done it before him if they had the sluggish Irish blood that seemed to gush and gurgle with restless achievement once they got away from the inertia of their own villages.

"Goodbye, darling, for now," said Derry. "Goodbye," she said, her head hiding in his chest.

"There you are," his father said, coming up with the slow loping stride of the shepherd. The dog was with him. He was a big loose-limbed man. In the moonlight you could mistake him for his son if his eyes weren't so quiet. Then where did Derry get the eyes? His mother below was a quiet-eyed woman too.

"There's a few people in below now," the father said. "We better go down to the house."

"I'll go down to them," said Derry. "Let ye come after me. I'll see ye below." And he was gone, bounding down the hill like a goat, sideways and forward and jumping and never missing a step. They stood and watched him becoming smaller and smaller.

"He has a lot of energy," said Derry's father.

"He has a lot of ambition," said Martha, moving off. He looked after her. She was probably crying, he thought. He knew Derry's mother was crying. He wondered idly if the tears of women would make a big river, all the tears of all the women in the world. What good did all those tears do ever? Did they ever soften a heart or deflect a man from a purpose, or if they did what did their success mean but frustration afterwards? He sighed and caught up with her.

"Going to America is not what it was when I was young," he said as he walked beside her. He admired Martha very much. She could walk down a hill like a healthy sheep.

"It's different," she said.

"Man," he said, "if you were going to America when I was young, you'd have to be preparing for a year. Everyone within fifty miles knew you were going, and they'd all make sure to see you before you left and wish you away with a tear or a little gift or a holy medal to guard you from the perils of the deep or a good scapular. Now, well look at it now."

"It's been pepped up," said Martha smiling. "Isn't it only twelve hours away? It's quicker now to go there than to go to Dublin."

"Spoiled they have it," he said. "Man, we used to have great times at the wakes before they went. We'd all cry our eyes out and we'd dance and drink porter until the small hours of the mornin'. I suppose you can't feel sorry for people now when they're only twelve hours away. Sure they could be only in the next parish."

"You'll miss Derry," she said.

He faltered then, of course.

"Oh, not much," he said. "It's like I'm saying. You haven't time. It's not the same. Besides, Derry was always restless. This is his third time away. Twice before, he was in England. He was always a restless one. I don't know where we got him.

Sometimes I say to his mother that she must have been courted by a wandering one on the sly." He chuckled at this. "You should have gone with him, Martha," he said then, gently. "He's very set on you."

"I'm set on him too," she said. "But I'm set on here. I think he should be ambitious at home. It would take little to make me go with him, but it will be better that I don't."

"I know him," said his father. "He will come back for you."

"Maybe by then," she said, "I will have changed, or he will have changed. Let him have his head now, and he will conquer the green hills of America."

"Will you come into the house?" he asked as they paused on the street. "A few of his friends and a few bottles of stout and a few songs. Man, but it's only a ghost of the good wakes long ago."

"I'll go home," she said. "We've said all that's to be said. I will see him when he comes home."

"All right. Good night, girl. God bless you."

He watched her away. She walked slowly, her head was bent. One hand was behind her holding her other arm. She was idly kicking small stones out of her way. He sighed and turned towards the door of his house. There was no noise coming from it. Somehow this annoyed him. He spoke out loud. "Man, years ago the roof would have been coming off that house with the noise," he said. He went in.

Derry came back for her. Almost a year to the day. But he didn't come alone. He was accompanied by two American sergeants and a firing party of American soldiers, and he had an American flag on his coffin, and his father had a medal that was given to Derry for bravery in some foreign war, and he was planted in the small graveyard halfway up the green hill, right beside the stream that roared when the rain hit the hill and tinkled when it was low. And from here if you stood by his grave to put fresh flowers in the glass jar, you could look out across the wide expanse of the sea; and if you had the vision, miles and miles and miles away you could see the green hills on the other side of the world.

Barney's Maggie

COLEMAN WAS GOING duck shooting because he wanted to be alone.

The reason he wanted to be alone was that he was very popular. He was twenty-four. He was very good-looking. He was just six foot tall and very well built. Even the old clothes he wore in the fields sat well on his body. His face was strong even though the cleft chin, the even white teeth, the straight nose, the long lashes and the blue eyes should have given his face the appearance of handsome weakness. They didn't. His fair hair curled. He had the kind of face and appearance you would have wished for yourself in your dreaming state when a good-looking woman would scorn you and you wished you were very attractive so that she would react like a dog at your heels. That was Coleman.

He could sing well and he could play the melodeon and he could dance. He was also a good man in a boat or behind the wheel of a tractor. It was impossible to be jealous of him. At least you had to force yourself to dislike him when you saw your best girl (as you thought) dancing with him at a hop in the parochial hall and looking up into his face with her eyes gleaming as if she had found the answer to prayer. After that, when he handed her back to you, he could disarm you with a genuine smile showing no trace of malice, but all the same ...

He liked to shoot at the end of the valley. He had a gun under his arm and he was his own retriever. There was a long field of oats there which had been cut and stooked, and the duck loved to flight into it of an autumn evening like now.

73

There was a good west wind and the sky was clear and was being almost tortured into colour by the setting sun. The field was a long way from the road where he left his bicycle, and he had to go up a winding road that led to Barney's house, and then jump a wall into the potato field, and after that cross a long stretch of field covered with gorse and bracken, and after that into a big field that was level and well walled and held good grass for the cattle that grazed it and he never gave a thought to Barney's bull until he heard the thundering behind him.

Bulls are very odd, particularly when they are a few years old. Only God in Heaven knows what figaries they take when a mood is on them. Why it should have come into the bull's head to suddenly take out after a harmless man going across the field with a shotgun under his arm, Coleman didn't know, and he didn't have time to think. He had time only to take to his heels and run towards the shelter of the far wall. He had no cartridges in his gun, and even if he had had he doubted if he could have turned in cold blood and shot the bull. Such thoughts were academic now because if he stopped to load it he would be dead. He was a fleet runner, but it dawned on him that the bull was fleeter and that it was very doubtful if he would reach the wall before the bull. He started to sweat. And a cold spot appeared between his shoulders where he expected to feel the blow, and he wondered if in a last desperate effort he would turn and smack at the bull with the butt of the gun. Then out of the corner of his eye he saw the figure of the girl coming over the wall with a stick in her hand. It was a very light stick. She ran towards him. He shouted, "Go back! Go back!" like a bloody grouse and he could feel that the bull was almost climbing up his back. He swore he could feel the breath of the snorting bull on the back of his neck. The wall seemed to be a mile away. And then the girl reached him and he stopped too. And there was the girl facing the bull. The bull paused, and that was his trouble. Before he could make up his mind the thin switch swished and his tender nose got a stroke of it. He dug in his forelegs and threw up his head. And he got another blow on the ringed nose and another and another, and then he turned, this bull did, and went off, and Coleman could have sworn that he had his tail between his legs. He was a big bull.

Coleman was ashamed and angry. "What did you do that for?" he asked. "I was only leading him on. In another minute I would have turned and given him a clout he never would forget."

"He was very near you," the girl said. "I was afraid he was going to puck you. He's been restless for the last few days."

Coleman looked at her. He knew her by sight. They had an expression in the place. They said: Such and such a thing is as ugly as Barney's Maggie. She was a tall girl, as tall as himself; and honestly the kindest thing you could say about her was that she had nice hair. It was a brown sort of crinkly hair. Her face would have looked well on a man, and the muscular neck and the heavy arms and thighs. She had a small nose, no notable eyelashes, heavy black eyebrows, and her teeth, though they were very white and shiny, were big teeth and a biteen irregular.

"I'm sorry if I interfered with your plans," she said. Her voice was serious.

Suddenly Coleman laughed. "Ah, to hell with it," he said. "I'll admit it. I was afraid of my life." Then he was serious. "Honest," he said, "if you hadn't come along that bastard might have killed me."

"That's nonsense," she said. "You would have done something."

"Well, I hope so," he said doubtfully.

"You're going shooting," she said. "This is a favourite place for you. I always see you this time of the year going up."

"That's right," he said. "Your father said I was welcome any time."

"You are," she said.

Her eyes were very clear. They didn't avoid his own. Many female eyes avoided his own when he looked into them.

"Well," he said, "that's that. Thanks. I better be going." He was surprised at himself. Anyone would think I was lost for words. "I'll see you again." And he climbed over the wall.

"Goodbye, Coleman," she said, and waved her arm, a large bare muscular arm.

He waved back and then headed towards the oatfield.

He was disturbed. There was a shake in his limbs. Well, anybody would be shaking after having a bull chasing him. He got to the field and he snuggled into a bunch of ferns near the wall and waited for the duck to flight. Now, he tried to think of any of the girls he knew and had loved hopping over a wall and hitting a bull on the snitch with a switch. He shook his head. They didn't measure up. Then, he thought, why do they say "as ugly as Barney's Maggie". She's well built all right. Not feminine, but she has nice clear brown eyes and nice hair, and I'll bet her skin is soft to the touch. He wondered was he thinking that way because she had more or less rescued him from the horns of a bull. No, he didn't think so, dammit. They shouldn't be allowed to talk about people like that. And then the six duck came in over him with whistling wings, and here he was dreaming and by the time he rose and shot they were away, and what should have been a perfect left and right was a flop. The duck were off and away with the drake cackling outrageously. And he was furious and he thought about her: I suppose she'll tell the whole bloody place about me and the bull and I'll be a laughing stock.

But she didn't.

He held his breath for a week or two after that, everywhere

he went; sitting on a stool in his favourite pub, cuddling his pint and waiting for the wag to start up about the livestock. But not a whisper. Well, at least, he thought, she is a very strange girl who can keep her mouth shut, a very strange girl; and he wondered why the look in her eyes had remained with him. It was ridiculous of course, but strange.

The next time he saw her was at the monthly fair. He was buying cattle himself and he was well dressed in a blue suit and a white collar and tie with his socks rolled over the bottoms of his trousers to save them from the dung. He knew somebody was looking at him for a long time (the way even the most stupid of us know) and he turned eventually seeking, and he saw her way up the street, looking at him. That's how tall she was that he could see her over the heads of the people. And just as if her eyes were a magnet he was drawn towards her, pushing his way through the throngs with his broad shoulders and never losing sight of her eyes. Then he was facing her. He couldn't credit the way his heart had speeded its beat. This was ridiculous. She wore an old raincoat and rubber boots. One hand was in her pocket and the other large hand held a switch, which he wondered about if it was the same one that she used on the bull.

"Hello, Maggie," he said, and wondered that he got pleasure out of pronouncing that very commonplace name.

"Hello, Coleman," she said. Then he forced himself from apologising to her because he had thought she was a loud mouth, and he said instead, "You have cattle?" "There they are," she said, pointing with the switch. And he looked at them, and there were three and they were good, small black mountain cattle but they were good, and he wanted to praise them. However, his native caution exerted itself, so he said, "They are not too bad," and she said, "They are very good." He said, "What are you asking for them?" and she said, "Fifty pounds each," and he laughed and said: "What? Are they filled with gold dust, or what?" And she said: "No, they are filled with meat and they are the best cattle in the fair." And he said: "If I didn't know you, I would say that you were crazy, but I'll give you forty for each of them," and she said: "You go to hell, Coleman, you know that they are worth more than that and even if I have to walk them home again I will do so." And oddly enough he was very pleased that she was bargaining, and it took him three-quarters of an hour to bring her down thirty shillings on each of them and they struck the bargain and he shook her hand. It was a hand as big and as firm and as muscular as his own, and he could only wonder again that the touch of it gave him pleasure. What's wrong with me? Am I cracked?

"Will you be going to the dance tonight?" he asked.

"Yes," she said. "I always go." He tried to think of the hall. He couldn't see her in it. Or could he? In the place where the ugly ones sat, just watching, sometimes being danced, most times not. He wondered that he could have been in the one hall with her and never have seen her.

"Good," he said, and they parted.

He looked forward to that dance. He wasn't questioning his behaviour any more. He just went with the flow. He saw her. She was well dressed, but unadorned, and he liked the look of her and he danced with her and she was light on her feet. He wanted to be with her all the time, but he struggled against this feeling and danced with the many pretty ones who enticed him; but he always went back to her, so that they said: Why is Coleman dancing so much with Barney's Maggie? It's not Lent, so he can't be doing penance. Maybe he's gone soft in the head. There was much tittering and speculation.

He knew the way she cycled home and he let her go and then he followed after her on his bicycle. They walked the four miles to the road that led to her home. It was a bright night. They didn't talk much, that was the odd thing; but before they finished the journey Coleman knew that he couldn't do without her. You'd have sworn that the fairies were working on him. But there it was and he couldn't but recognise it.

There on the road, he didn't even kiss her. He held her hand and before he left her he rubbed one of his palms on her hair and down the side of her cheek, making her close her eyes and tremble. Her skin was as soft as satin, as he knew it would be, and he said: "Listen, Maggie, on Friday night next I will come up to the house and I will talk to your father." That's what he said, completely committed. She knew it and he knew it but there was nothing they could do about it. He even felt a little that she didn't want or require this feeling that was flooding her that could have only one end. But what could they do? They were both realists and it had to be faced.

Coleman expected to wake up in the morning with misery flooding him and he groaning, What have I done? Why did I say I would be up on Friday to ask for her? But he didn't feel that way. He felt, Thank God and I might have so easily passed her by, and why am I so lucky and how is it that some other scut hadn't seen the worth of her before and robbed me?

Friday before the journey he went into his pub to get a pint. He had been working hard all day in the fields and he wanted a pint. He was cleaned up and shone like a pair of shoes. He had never been so particular with his appearance.

He drank alone as he was sometimes known to do, and the conversation of the two other men there did not percolate into his mind until the one sentence out of their conversation hit him, probably because the speaker was emphasising it with blows on the counter. "... as mad," he was saying, "as mad as Barney's Joe! That's what I'm telling you. He was as mad as Barney's Joe." That played a rhythm in his head: "As ugly as

Barney's Maggie; as mad as Barney's Joe." Could that be the same Barney? he wondered. What did they mean? Barney lived so far out in the valley that he didn't know much about them. He knew Barney just to see, and Maggie; and he remembered from way back at school, wasn't it, that Barney had a son, or had he?

He turned.

"Who's this you say, Rino?" he asked the man. "Who's this Joe of Barney? Has he a bad temper?"

Rino laughed.

"Where were you, Coleman?" he asked. "That's the Barney that has the ugly daughter. You know. The one up the valley. His son, that is. His son Joe. Mad as a hare. Five years back. Maybe you weren't here. Was that the time you went to Liverpool to change your watch?"

"No," said Coleman, "that was the time I went to Scotland to dig spuds."

"Anyhow," said Rino, "Joe went off his top. They had to tie him up. You know. He never went to school much. Always a bit weak upstairs but a fine man. Lord, he was as big as a house. Listen, I was talking to a fellow from the asylum. He was talking about Joe. He gets bad sometimes. They have to put him in the padded place. Then they take him out. He watches the door, see. If there are only two of them, he attacks them straight away and nearly murders them. But if they send four for him, he counts them and smiles and goes with them. Isn't that the cute fellow? Oh, you should see him. Shoulders like the width of a double door, but no brain at all. That's Barney's Joe. That's why they say it."

"I see," said Coleman, and his blood ran cold. He left the pint there and went out into the evening. He walked clear of the village and he climbed into the hills and he sat there on the heather, looking down. He could see the white road going back into Maggie's valley. That changes everything, even a flooding feeling. Why hadn't she said something about this? Did she have time to say anything? She didn't. How many times had he talked to her at all? Very few before he was swamped. Suppose she knew that he knew like everyone knew that she had a brother who was a nut. What was he going to do? What in the name of God was he going to do? He knew what he should do. He should say to hell with them and he should get down soon onto the white road. He could imagine her up in the house waiting for him and her father waiting for him. The preparations for him. How she would be feeling. So what did he do? He went back into the village and he went into the pub and he got rotten stinking drunk. That's what he did. And that night was remembered for a long time. They spoke of it afterwards as the night Coleman got drunk. Rino, bewildered, would never forget it. He was beaten into unconsciousness by Coleman, for which assault Coleman was afterwards fined and bound to the peace.

But nobody ever knew how Coleman felt when he awoke the next morning. He awoke and said: "Oh, God, I have ruined my life." And he hurriedly dressed and he mounted his bicycle and he went up the valley and left his bicycle and climbed the road to her house. He went in the open door. Only she was there in the kitchen with the twig in her hand sweeping the hearth and she saw him, and he looked into her eyes and he knew it was no good, no good at all. Just one look and he knew it was no good, just like before one look and he knew that he loved her.

No talk at all. No talk. He just turned out with his shoulders bowed and came back to the valley.

He's much older now and his curly hair is very grey and he is a very hard worker and people like him a lot, but many disappointed hearts still wonder why Coleman never married. Never at all. Now you know.

The Sailor

———————◇———————

I FIRST MET the Sailor the morning after the night we celebrated Jingo getting his second Medical. Jingo and I had started medicine seven years ago. I was doing my final next year. It took Jingo the seven years to reach the second. Jingo didn't mind. The first seven years are the hardest, Jingo said. His father, a farmer in Roscommon, swore his oath that he would make a doctor out of Jingo if it killed him or Jingo or his bank manager.

Everyone liked Jingo. The examiners would have been only too happy to pass Jingo. Everyone was for him. Everyone said if only he could get his exams he would make a great doctor. When the news spread that Jingo had got his second, every one nearly broke out flags. Great news, everyone said; now if he can do the next four years in eight, it will be all right. He was everybody's friend.

Except mine. I hated Jingo at this moment as we walked home in the cold dawn. Jingo was humming. All the singing was in my head. I wanted to be sick. Jingo's freckles stood out on his pale face. His eyes were as clear as if he had had twelve hours' sleep. He shoved out his chest. He banged it. "It's a great morning," Jingo said. "Doesn't it make you feel good to be alive on a morning like this?" He sucked the cold ozone into his lungs. He didn't even cough.

"The curse of the God of drunkards on you, Jingo," I said.

"What's wrong, Mac?" he asked, clapping me vigorously on the back. "Pain in the craw, boy? What you want is a cure."

"Please, Jingo," I said, "don't strike me. Don't talk about

cures. I want to go home and be sick and go to bed."

"Bags," said Jingo. "Have to have a cure."

"Where do we get a cure," I asked, "at five-thirty in the morning? Aren't we after being forcibly ejected from three pubs since midnight? I just want to go home, Jingo. I'm sorry I ever met you. I'm sorry you ever got your second Med. I hope you never get another exam or, if you do, that I am in China when you get it."

"My God, you are bad," said Jingo. "Never mind. We'll rattle up the Sailor. The Sailor is a good sport. The Sailor'll give us a cure."

He turned away from the promenade beside the sea where we walked in toward the cluster of the town. The dawn was looking at us from over the sea with a cold steely eye. Every time I put my feet on the pavement somebody hit me on the head with a mallet.

Into the town we went and over the way and down by a row of shops facing the river. He stopped at a door there. He raised a knocker and banged loudly.

"S-sh, for God's sake!" I said. The knocker reverberated again.

"The Sailor won't mind," said Jingo. "The Sailor is a good sport."

I wondered why Jingo had lived so long. That was his way. The direct approach. You either murdered him or gave in to him.

A window shot up. A large bald head with ruffled grey hair around the fringes all tossed. A red face with a heavy grey moustache. Two red eyes glaring down at us.

"Ah, Sailor, me oul pal," said Jingo up to him. "Let us in for the love of God and give us a cure. We're corpsed."

"Where the hell do ye think this is?" the Sailor asked in a rich booming voice. "D'ye think this is Lourdes?"

"Ha, ha, ha," said Jingo, heartily. "'At's a boy."

The eyes looked at me. "That thing looks dying anyhow,"

said the Sailor. "All right, Jingo, I'll let ye in when I get into me drawers." The window banged down.

"There you are," said Jingo. "Didn't I tell you?" I was too far gone to rejoin. I leaned against the wall. Jingo had to shake me out of a sleep to get me in the door. It was a small pub, one of these nice unfashionable ones where you sat on a barrel or stood on your legs and felt at home. The Sailor was a vast man. The ceiling wasn't low but he wasn't very far away from it. His bulk was huge, emphasised by the stripes in his shirt shoved into his pants.

"A nice bloody hour of the mornin'," he was grumbling as he pulled the corks, "to get a fella out of his bed. Somebody'll slaughter you some day, Jingo."

"More power to them," said Jingo. "Did you hear I got me exam, Sailor?"

"I did," said the Sailor. "A bloody miracle, I said, when I heard it. You must have somebody prayin' for you."

"It's brain," said Jingo, "pure brain. Here's to all the sailors that go down on the vasty deep." He swallowed his beer.

A small boy with fair curly hair came out of the inside door then. He had a bucket of hot ashes. It was heavy for him.

"Will I throw them into the river for you now, Grandfather?" he asked.

"No, no, Paddo," said the Sailor lifting the flap and coming out. "I'll do that meself. You'd be frizzled."

"Hello, Paddo," said Jingo.

"Hello, Jingo," said Paddo. "What ye doin' in at this hour?"

"We came to see the doctor," said Jingo. "He's the medicine man. Giving us medicine he is."

"That's not medicine," said Paddo. "That's beer."

"Out of the mouths of babes and sucklings," said Jingo.

"Don't mind him, Paddo," said the Sailor going out with the bucket. I watched him cross the road and empty it over the low wall into the river. The light ashes rose in a cloud. Then he came back. He was a very big man, moving ponderously. Jingo had Paddo up on the counter. He was a nice little boy, about five years old. Jingo was drawing faces for him in the spilled beer on the counter. Jingo had a way with kids too.

The Sailor came back and closed the door.

"That fella," he said to me, "will get his last exam the day I put ass or tip in the Atlantic Ocean." He went in behind the counter. This remark interested me.

"Do you like the sea?" I asked.

He looked closely at me. Then he relaxed and came over.

"Why do you think they call me the Sailor?" he asked.

"Presumably," I said, "because you were."

"No," he said. "That's what they are like around here. They always name you the opposite of what you are. I never put a foot in the sea in me life and I never will."

"Why?" I asked.

"It's easy," he said. "I was born way out beyant where they live by boats. I saw me father come back one time on two planks and a belly of sea water in him. I had one brother that never came back at all, and an uncle." He paused then. I could see that picture clearly. "I said I would never let the sea get me. So I came into this town. I worked in a shop. Then I started this place of me own. Where could you get farther from the sea than here?"

"I see what you mean," I said. He rubbed the counter with a cloth.

"I have three sons," he said then. "One of them is Paddo's father, the eldest one. What do you think they went and did?"

"They went to sea," I said.

"That's right," he said. "They did. One of them into your men's navy, and the other two fish the bay out there in their boats. So you see, I warned them. I told them. But they wouldn't listen. They are safe so far. But it won't get me. You understand that. You get my point, mister."

"I do," I said. I did. He is a nice man, the Sailor. Why does or how does Jingo get to know only the real nice people? I felt I had known the Sailor for years. The Sailor was Biblical. In a few sentences he told you the story of his life and it was all there in a clear honest face.

"So long, Paddo," Jingo was saying. "If I had a bob I'd give it to you; but I have no money and my friend there has to pay for the medicine and he has no money left."

"Yes I have," I said. "I have ninepence. Here, Paddo, here's ninepence and don't go buying boats with it. Right?" I inquired of the Sailor.

"Right, mister," said the Sailor. He smiled a big smile at me. I felt that we were friends. I felt I had really had a cure. We went home to bed.

I was going out of the hospital getting into my coat. I had a date. I was late for my date. She was redheaded and punctual. "Doctor," said the Sister stopping me. "An emergency. Down near the boats. They are putting oxygen into the ambulance."

I said a bad word.

"Tut, tut," she said. "Only six months qualified and he talks like a doctor already."

I ran for the ambulance. I was fuming. I was thinking about the temper of my redhead and how she could scorch you with silence or speech.

We went through the town fast. We went down to the fishing-boat quays. I was still thinking of myself. There was a crowd down there. They looked around as the ambulance stopped. I went through them. Jingo was bending over the body of the boy on the ground. He looked up at me. His eyes were very sad.

"It's Paddo," he said. "Poor oul Paddo."

The fair hair was clinging to the narrow face. All the water was out of him. He was wearing a red jersey that was dark in colour from the water. Short pants and his legs and feet bare and brown.

"We'll try the oxygen on him," I said.

"It's no use," said Jingo, bending and taking the light body up into his arms. "I was coming home from college. I've been at him ever since. They were playing in the boats. He fell over. They didn't miss him until it was too late."

The tide was in. It was a high tide. It was bearing the black boats high. It was calm sea and clear, the top of it littered with things it picked up as it came in.

"He was the nicest little fella I ever met," said Jingo moving toward the ambulance.

He stopped there as the Sailor came through the crowd. He looked into Jingo's eyes. Jingo was too late hiding the look in them. The Sailor came over. He looked down into the hanging face of the dead boy. He put out an enormous hand and laid it gently on the smooth skin of the boy's face.

"Oh, Paddo, Paddo," said the Sailor, and great gobs of tears poured out of his eyes like rainwater on a pane of glass.

"Get him in, Jingo," I said becoming official.

Jingo brought him in and placed him on the stretcher. "You can come," I said to the Sailor. That broke a lot of rules.

We went away.

Jingo and he sat on the other side as I put the oxygen mask on the boy's face. I heard the Sailor sobbing.

"Shush! Shush!" said Jingo.

He quieted down. I pumped oxygen into the small frame. I knew it was no good. He was too dead.

"Ye don't know why I cry," said the Sailor. "I don't cry for the reason ye think. I cry because I am a selfish man. I love my Paddo, better than my own sons, and here I look at him now and ye know the thought that comes to me. It is a terrible thought. Always I have been afraid of the sea. Some day, I say, the sea will get you. I say it will never get me, but deep inside here I am afraid of this. The jinx is on me. And now the sea gets Paddo and I think, Well, that's what it is. The sea takes Paddo and it will not take you. Christ forgive me for a sinful man."

"Shush, man, you're wild, you're wild," said Jingo.

"I think I must tell his mother. I must tell his father. I see their faces falling to pieces like limestone under a sledge. I think of me empty life without that fair laughing boy in it, and at the end of my thinking there is the other thought. You have paid off the sea with Paddo."

"For God's sake, Sailor!" Jingo shouted.

The oxygen ruffled the fair drying hair of the boy.

It was six o'clock in the morning. It was a cold bitter morning. I couldn't look the morning in the face unless I half closed my eyes. We were walking home, Jingo and I.

Jingo was as sober as a judge. (Has this wise saw ever been physically tested?) The reason Jingo was as sober as a judge was that he was drinking orange crushes.

"Here, Mac," said Jingo, "gimme your hand." I didn't, he took it. He rubbed the palm of my hand against his coat. "You have now the honour," he said, "to be rubbing Doctor Jingo."

"Oh, God," I said, "my head."

"Do you remember, Mac, the time I got my second Med, we walked along this way, you and I, after celebrating?"

"How can I remember that far back?" I asked. "That must be eight years ago. All I remember about that morning is hoping that I'd be in China if ever the day came that you got your final."

The odd part of this was that I was in China. I had been a doctor on a boat for two years. I was in China until two months ago. I come home to the home town for a brief holiday, and what happens? I walk into Jingo's final.

"What you want is a cure," said Jingo, "and I know the very man who will give us a cure."

"The Sailor," I said.

"The very man," said Jingo.

"How is the Sailor?" I asked.

"The Sailor is not the man you knew," said Jingo. "I say the Sailor, and you remember a huge man who would shake floor-boards."

"No," I said, "I remember a big man crying over the body of a boy."

"So you hadn't forgotten," he said.

"There are some things, Jingo," I said, "that you never forget."

"Well," he said, "I see the Sailor very often ever since. How many years ago is that? Say four. Every year that passes the Sailor has become four times smaller. Wait until you see him."

"I think I'd like to not see him," I said. "I think I'd prefer to remember him as he was."

"You know the fixation he had," said Jingo. "About the sea. About Paddo taking the curse from him. He was always such an honest man. There isn't a sinner in the town now who hasn't been told what a scoundrel he is. Over several balls of malt. The Sailor has taken to the drink."

"Let's go home another way, Jingo," I said. "Let's not pass by the Sailor's."

"No," said Jingo. "I promised him. The day I got the final I was to go to him until he rubbed my coat."

We turned the corner. I was thinking out of the past of the Sailor emptying the ashes in the river and coming back and saying something about Jingo getting his final exams the day he dipped ass or tip in the sea.

"There he is," said Jingo pointing.

The light was in the sky. Away in the distance we saw the figure of the man leaving his door and going over to the wall with the bucket in his hand. Even from here the change in him shocked me. He was a small man. He didn't walk ponderously with weight, but slowly with bowed age.

We walked faster.

We saw him raise the bucket and swing it and the cloud of ashes leaving, and then the bucket didn't come back but went on and the little man's legs went over the low stone wall and he followed the bucket into the river.

Jingo ran. I ran. I had to close my eyes. The pounding of my feet was exploding in my head. It was a very swift river and very deep. It turned left at the bridge and joined the sea. We ran toward the junction. Jingo was far ahead of me. I saw him flinging his coat away and leaping over the wall. I shouted "Jingo, for God's sake, come back!"

I ran on. My heart was bursting. Inside the bridge there was a round where the wall of the river met the wall of the sea. It was grass covered. I threw myself full length on it. I saw Jingo to my left in the water. He breathed deep and dived. I saw his taut wet trousers as he went under. He came up again.

"I have him," he said pulling at something.

I held out my hand.

"Catch, catch, Jingo," I shouted, "for the love of God!" I didn't look to the right. Here the sea and the stream of the main river were meeting and clashing. It was a maelstrom there. Every time the sea came in, it was like that. A terrible lashing of white foam. If Jingo gets into that he will have been a doctor for a day. His wet hand caught mine as he was being swept past. I held it with my hand. I held it with my two hands.

"He's slipping, slipping, slipping," Jingo shouted. "Let me go. Let me go, Mac."

I didn't let him go. I held on with my two hands. Out of the corner of my eye I saw a mass of white and black that rose to the surface of the thrashing water and then sank as it swept into the stream. Jingo was like a big fish on the end of a weak line. If I let him go he would never come back. He shouted up at me, his teeth bare, gripping. He tried to strike up at my face with his free hand. I held on to him with my eyes closed. After a time he became quiet. He reached his free hand for the top of the quay wall. I rose to my knees. He came free. The water dripped from him. His freckles stood out on his pale face. He walked past me. He ran to the middle of the bridge. He looked where the river had been conquered by the sea.

The sea was retreating after its ephemeral victory. It was carrying booty with it.

"How right he was," said Jingo. "How right he was."

He rested his head on his clenched hands.

The Hurling Match

——◆——

"T WISTER," SAID FINBAR, "you'll have to help me."
"Sit down, man," said Twister. "Don't be so worked up. You'll die young. Have a pint."

"Oh, no," said Finbar. "I never drink it. I'll have a glass of lemonade."

"You'll die even younger," said Twister. "Here, Jack," he shouted to the assistant who was very busy. "Put a clothespeg on your nose and pour out a glass of lemonade for my friend. Now, Finbar, what's the trouble?"

Finbar was fidgety. He looked incongruous sitting on the shiny seat of the snug. Too big and throbbing with muscle and tanned by the sun. He was very young, Twister thought. He had red hair and two darting, green eyes.

"It's the hurling club," he said.

"What's wrong with it?" Twister asked. "Is somebody going to steal it on you?"

"You think that's funny," said Finbar, "but honest to God that's what it amounts to. You know the brothers?"

"I do," said Twister. Everybody knew the three of them. The three F's, they called them: Finbar, Fergus and Fiacra. Their father was a notorious patriot and he had declaimed when they were born that he was going to bring them up to be Irish to the marrow even if he had to kill them. Before they were weaned he had fashioned hurley sticks for them, and now they were the three best hurlers in the country.

"Well," said Finbar. "Two years ago I had a row with them and I left their club. It's a good club. You know that."

"It is," said Twister. "They have more medals than an Irish champion dancer."

"All right," said Finbar. "They won the county championship four years in a row. I was fed up with them. Just because I was a few years younger, they treat me like a schoolboy, so I say I'll show them, and I go out and from our street I build up a team and I tell them that I'll bate the socks off them, I'll show them; and I would, too, only every time we have somebody really good on the team the two brothers come and flatter him and give him a new jersey and togs and maybe boots, too, if he is really good and a new hurley stick so all the time I am like a fella pouring water into a jug that has a hole in the bottom of it, and if only I could give them all free jerseys and togs and boots and hurleys I'd be able to hold them together for a few years and as sure as you're there, Twister, I'd end up beating the brothers' team and taking the county championship. But yesterday they got my best man and we have to play them next Saturday in the second round of the championship and they have me whipped a cripple, and if there was only some way I could think of getting money and holding what we have, maybe next year we would wallop them. I'd love to see their faces if we walloped them. I'd just love to see their faces. I thought you know such a lot about making money that you could think of some way, Twister, some way at all."

Twister was flattered. He rarely played games. It required too much energy. If you could earn sixpence for every drop of sweat it might be a paying proposition, but just to use up all that energy for nothing, didn't make sense. Looking at two teams playing always pained him. The game of hurling seemed particularly designed to waste energy. It was as old as Ireland — older. It was old as the ash tree from which the hurleys were shaped. They were made long and slender about three to four feet in length. They were slender to fit into the palms and then widened out to a thick boss, wide and curved to the natural grain of the wood. The ball was as thick as a medium-sized fist made of thick leather with a hard core. The leather cover was cut like two figure eights and sewed together leaving the double-thick ridges. When it was hit with the wide boss of the hurley, the natural spring in the ash could send it great distances. There were fifteen men on each side. The goal posts were tall. Anything under the bar of the posts was a goal. Anything over the bar was a point. A goal was equal to three points and great energy was wasted trying for goals. There was a goalkeeper to stop goals if he could. In front of the goalie there were six backs to defend him, three fullbacks and three halfbacks. In center were two midfield men who tried to feed the ball to the forwards who worked in front of the opponents' goal. There were three full-forwards and three half-forwards. It was amazing how much energy skilled men could waste with the ball. They could stop it as it flew through the air, deflect it and send it back. They could assist it on its way with a beautifully timed stroke. Sometimes two men might assist it on its way at the same time and there would be a clash and smash of hurleys and it was a brave sound to hear. The best hurlers had to be light of foot and quick of eye, like dancers. Twister really thought of all the beauty of its playing as waste.

"Well, Finbar," he said. "Your problem is very simple. All you do is have a challenge game, charge a shilling a skull, and get twenty or thirty pounds!"

"Listen, Twister," said Finbar. "No man in this town will pay a shilling at the gate when he can get in over the wall."

"Very dishonest," said Twister. "You say you have no chance of beating the brothers' team next Saturday?"

"Not a hope in hell," said Finbar.

"That's good," said Twister. "Now suppose you asked me to referee the game. Could you do that?"

"You know about hurling? I suppose we could. Everybody

knows you. What good would that do?"

"You'd be surprised," said Twister. "Are there any club funds at all?"

"About three pounds," said Finbar.

"That'll do," said Twister. "I'll risk two pounds of my own money on the deal and call on your three pounds after the game, if it is necessary. I don't think it will be. Go home now, Finbar, and limber up and call out the team and practise assiduously until Saturday, and you might be surprised at the results."

"Honest, Twister," Finbar said wide-eyed. "Are you up to something?"

"I am merely on the side of justice," said Twister. "Make sure I am appointed referee and leave the rest to God."

Finbar left with hope in his breast.

Twister went up the town and into the small, square park where he knew that he would find Charity Charlie. Charlie always spent about an hour a day in the park. Half an hour before going to his office in the morning, and half an hour after closing it in the afternoon. He was a bookmaker and he wasn't charitable, but on the rather rare occasions when he was paying out on a winning horse he would always mumble, "Charity! Charity!" so that the happy person didn't know whether Charlie was chiding them or praising them for taking his money.

He was there all right, sitting on his usual seat looking blankly at the sky. He was a large, fat man. He had a lot of his own hair still, and never wore a hat. His shirt collar was always crumpled because it had a hard task trying to encircle his neck. You could never know what colour suit he wore because he always had it covered by an old tweed coat, buttoned tightly across his stomach. He was very dark and he should have shaved twice a day and only shaved once so he always looked as if he wanted a shave. And always, always there was a cigarette between his lips. His look was blank and incurious but everybody knew that he was as cute as a hawk.

"Hello, Charlie," said Twister sitting beside him and hitting him on the round shoulders. "How are you, Charlie?"

Charlie looked at him out of the incurious eyes and grunted.

He didn't like Twister. Twister had been disliked so often by many people that he was no longer affected by it. Charlie had cause to dislike him. Twister didn't put money on horses often, but when he did, he had a terrible habit of backing the right horse, say seven times out of ten. That would have been all right, if he only backed himself but when he thought he was right he generally went into Charlie's shop followed by about ten favoured citizens who backed where he backed and when they duly got their winnings, handed over ten per cent to Twister, more or less cheerfully. This pay-off was always done in the bookie's shop where Charity could see it happening, and it must have been a sore sight for him seeing his easily earned money going into the pocket of Twister.

"It's a great day, thank God," said Twister. "It's a wonderful thing to feel the June sun on your face."

Charlie grunted. It was a cautious grunt. He was running over in his mind some of the reasons there might be for Twister accosting him. They were all bad.

"You know a lot about hurling teams, Charlie," said Twister. "I'm told you're the principal authority in this town."

Charlie was just a little flattered. "Huh," he said.

"You know Finbar Daly and the two brothers? They have two teams."

"Pats and Joes," said Charlie.

"Which is the best?" Twister asked.

"Pats," said Charlie. "Best in the country, best in the county. No beating them."

"I think you're wrong," said Twister.

Charlie looked at him. "Buzz," he said. It was a scornful noise.

"All right," said Twister. "I was down looking at the young team the other day – Finbar's – the Joes. I think they're better than anybody thinks. I think when they play the Pats next Saturday that they'll knock hell out of them."

"Buzz, buzz!" Charlie ejaculated. It was a double-scornful noise.

Twister pretended to be angry.

"Well, I don't goddam think that you're such a goddam expert as everybody thinks," Twister said hotly. "You're just way out. You sink back into a reactionary just because they've been winning for four years or so. You think they can't be whacked. I say they can."

"Go to hell," said Charlie. His neck was getting red.

"A fine expert," said Twister. "I tell you you haven't seen these other young fellas. I tell you they'll run the legs off them. You ought to see them!"

"Don't have to," said Charlie warmly. "Bunch of schoolboys. Damn. Jam pot!"

"Condemned unseen," said Twister rising from the seat. "Boy, there's an expert! Sitting on his seat and everything is supposed to stay the same way forever because he says so."

"Six to one," Charlie ground out between his teeth and his cigarette.

"All right," he said. "I'll have five pounds on it. I'll show you!"

"All right." Charlie rubbed his shoe on the gravel. "Buzz!"

Twister walked away in high dudgeon, until he was out of sight, and then he relaxed and walked down the town smiling largely.

Charlie scuffed the gravel for some time until his anger waned, then he started to think and an empty feeling came into the pit of his stomach.

"Caught again," said Charlie. "Charity!"

It was a very beautiful day. The field was by the shore. There was a high wall all around except on the side near the sea, so it was only simpletons who paid at the gate. All the other spectators walked by the seashore as if they were out for their health and then they turned into the playing field as if by accident. There was a good attendance. If there was no charge at the gate, there wouldn't have been half as many of them.

Twister blew his whistle importantly.

All around the field the teams were changing hurriedly from clothes into togs. The Pats wore green and white jerseys and the Joes wore blue. The colours were in honour of St Patrick and St Joseph. Some of them were on the field already. The hurleys flashed as they swung them, the air swishing as it was cut. Twister blew the whistle again.

The teams lined up.

Pats looked very well. They all wore jerseys and togs and boots. Of the fifteen of them, ten were taller than Twister and he wasn't small. Fergus and Fiacra Daly were terrible big – muscles bulging on their legs and arms. The Joes were a sorry sight, Twister thought. Only some of them had togs and some of them jerseys and a few of them boots. Some of them were playing in their bare feet. It's a good job they have me as referee, Twister was thinking. Still, they were young and active and some of them were big, and the only thing that was wrong with them was an inferiority complex. To his surprise Finbar looked very happy. He kept waving cheerfully at Twister. This worried Twister. It's all right him having faith in me, Twister thought, but he should wait until the game is over. Then he became more cheerful when he saw the squat, watching figure of Charity Charlie, standing on the sideline with a blue curl of cigarette smoke rising from him. Twister chuckled. He called for the ball. He hefted the hard leather in his hand, blew the whistle and threw it at the waiting hurleys.

The backs went back, the forwards scuffled and before Twister had time to look around him, Fiacra Daly had hit the ball a terrible puck and it flew toward the Joes' goal and nobody could stop it and there it was, a goal – three points!

Twister was indignant. The Pats were jubilant in a superior, indifferent way.

Twister blew again. The goalie hit the ball out. It soared again to Fergus Daly, who reached high and caught it and hit it back up to his forward line. Fiacra caught it up there and it was being banged in for another goal when the referee's whistle blew.

There was pandemonium.

Twister was immediately surrounded by all of the Pats team waving hurleys in his face. "Hey, Twister, what the hell's the idea? What the hell do you think you're doing? What's the bloody idea?" and also many ruder things which Twister ignored completely. He just walked with dignity up the field and called for the ball and indicated a free puck out for the Joes. There was murder again. There was scuffling on the sideline as the partisans argued it out. Fergus Daly was bending over Twister, as if he was going to eat him.

"All right," said Twister. "Do you want to be put off the field?"

Fergus had to subside. Finbar was pulling at Twister's sleeve, saying in a sort of stage whisper, "Hey, Twister, it's all right. It's all right." Twister shook him off and restarted the game.

Well, he disorganised the Pats, there's no doubt about that. Up to the end of the first half he had given fourteen frees against them for imaginary infringements. Since a free meant that you could take an unopposed shot at your opponent's goal, the Joes had scored ten points and a goal as practically free gifts, and since he had the power, he further weakened the opposition by ordering three of the Pats' best hurlers off the playing field for using threatening language. If you do things, Twister thought, you must do them well or not at all, and even with the help he was giving the Joes they were only three points in the lead. One disturbing thing that happened was that Charlie came on the field at the interval and for the first time in Twister's memory of him he was without a fag stuck in his mouth and he seemed to be wiping tears out of his eyes. Twister hoped they were tears of rage and frustration. "Buzz, Twister," he said, sort of choking. "I haven't seen a game like this for thirty years. It's murder!"

Twister whistled up the second half.

There was no doubt he had fifteen bitter enemies with hurleys in their hands. He wasn't exactly afraid, although he agreed in his mind that in theory a strong man like himself could hold and control fifteen strong men. But to be in there in the middle of them and smelling the sweat and seeing them glaring at him with red eyes was a different proposition.

By reputation he was a dangerous man to tangle with for he knew all the wrong ways of fighting and he was reputed to have a long memory and to have always succeeded in getting his own back like the elephant, but he reflected now that people might forget all these things when the blood was heated and that he better proceed with caution. So he allowed Pats to bang in two goals and three points before he started to whistle them up again and to organise the play so that the ball could get down to Finbar who was unbeatable with a ball in his hand. But even so, at the very end, the Pats were leading by a few points and just before the final whistle could blow, the whole team of them seemed to be overcome by a red-rioting frenzy. They lashed the ball here, there and everywhere when they got it and when they hadn't, they lashed the air or a few shins or banged their hurleys so that they sunk inches into the ground and they cursed and swore and the ball flew so fast from here to there that it beat his eyes and worse his whistle.

There was an awful roar of anguish going up from all sides, from players and spectators. Everyone was shouting and arguing and groups were gathering and exchanging blows, so then Twister blew the whistle for full time and as far as he could remember, Pats had won the game despite his best efforts and he only blew because the whole thing was suddenly giving him butterflies in the stomach. He felt that he had been for the past hour putting TNT into a big bomb and that if he didn't stop the bomb would explode and the minute he blew the long blast, he knew he had done the wrong thing because the bomb exploded.

He was in the middle of the field and the whole of the two teams were running toward him with their hurleys waving and behind them came a phalanx of the spectators waving their fists and shouting. He reflected that there wasn't really time to argue reasonably and quietly with them. He saw himself being beaten into a bloody pulp on the grass of the field, so he did the only thing anyone could do, he took to his heels and ran like hell. There was only one place to run and that was the opening where the sea met the shallow river. He felt hurt that the Joes should have turned against him as well as the Pats, and he reflected bitterly that as far as the spectators went, those who pay least criticise most, and that they had no common right to be enraged and about how true the proverb was that the best hurlers are on the fence and what hurt him most was that it was all perfectly legal, and the referee was the man who should be obeyed.

It was Finbar who held them back long enough to let him get into the river.

He blocked them with his hurley, shouting, but they went around him and he was thrown out of the way and then they just stood on the bank and pelted a few stones after Twister and then the sight of him up to his knees in muddy ooze and then falling forward and getting wet and rising again changed their anger to jeers and sneers that were even harder to bear, and when he got to the middle of the river, he braced himself against the swift flow of the current and from here endeavoured by word of mouth to defend his actions and to berate them for ingratitude and to tell them that they would all be fired out of the Association when his report was sent in to the proper authorities.

Charity Charlie was on the bank, too. He was laughing. It was the first time in history anybody had ever seen his teeth.

Twister told him this, among other things. "Listen, Twister," Finbar shouted. "Don't be calling Charlie names. Charlie is giving the Joes jerseys and togs all around for free. Isn't he decent? He told us that before the game. As long as the Pats beat us fair and square. He said not to tell you. He wanted to surprise you. Isn't he damn decent?"

Twister thought of his hour of torture and in vain, organised by that cunning excrescence. His language was frightful. He started to wade back to get his hands on Charlie and crucify him but the sight of Finbar's big brothers still foaming at the mouth, deterred him, so he ruined his clothes wading across the river and pulling himself up on to the high stone quay and he remained there for some time with indecent reflections until the others had drifted away from the opposite side, all except Charlie who had lighted a cigarette and sat on the bank in the sun and kept looking over at Twister with great enjoyment.

Before departing, stiff-legged, Twister shouted across at him.

"Goddam you, Charity," he shouted. "I'll never bring you another bit of business. Never again!"

Duck Soup

———————————◇———————————

THE WHOLE THING was unsavoury from beginning to end.

None of it would have happened if Gaeglers hadn't taken into his head to go for a walk. It confirmed him in his opinion ever afterwards that walking was dangerous. It was a delightful autumn evening. It was about eight o'clock. The sea was calm. The sun was going down peacefully; the air was warm and all the colours in the sky were friendly, so, obeying an impulse – a rare occurrence with Gaeglers – he turned his face towards the seashore and the promenade. He felt well. He had enjoyed his supper. He was freshly shaved; his neat blue suit was new, the open collar of his spotlessly white shirt showed his neck and throat to be nicely tanned by the sun and he enjoyed but did not encourage the many passing female glances cast at his handsome face and his dark curly hair.

Also he had money in his pocket, so he was more or less at peace with the world.

He walked out and out. There was a lot of people on the lower end of the promenade, and the silent sea reflected the lights of the coloured bulbs strung from the electric-light poles, and its immense body also threw back or carried away the exaggerated noise of the loud-speakers that brayed jazz tunes from the gaily lighted fun fair; chair-o-planes twirling and girls screaming deliciously and swing boats and the spit and thunder of the dodgem cars. All very nice and strictly for juveniles, Gaeglers thought as he passed by, although in the thick of the tourist season he had found it a fertile acre for simple people who were willing to give him money so that he could live and enjoy his simple pleasures. Ah, yes, Gaeglers thought with a smile.

Farther back, there were no coloured bulbs and in the darker places the seats were occupied by couples who had merged themselves almost into one. Occasionally they turned romantically lighted faces towards the calm sea or the coloured sky. True love, Gaeglers thought, and he also thought of what it would lead to; smelly prams and screaming kids and being behind with the rent and uneconomic living and good looks and perfume turning to slatternly appearance and stale Woodbine smoke.

Farther back it was darker still and he felt better. No artificial light with its feeble challenge to the light of the sky. Just one or two lights reflecting down in narrow beams onto the white concrete paths. He walked to where the promenade ended, paused awhile to look at the sea and the lights dying out in the sky and the thirty-second light flashing in the bay, and then he turned for home.

He was hardly on his way when he heard the footsteps behind him, and a hand hit him on the back and a thin voice said, "Hello, Gaeglers!" If he wasn't feeling peaceful he would have hit the owner of the hand because he hated to be touched. He stopped. There were two of them and the sight of them dimmed his spirits. They were two brothers, tall and thin and dressed in brown suits. They were twins, people said, and they were named Spares. That was their father's name. They were known as Twotees. One was Tom and the other Toby, so if you wished to distinguish them, which nobody really wished to do, the fellow with the mole over his right eyebrow was Twotee Tee and the other one was Twotee To. Mainly everybody wished they had never been born and saw no reason for their present existence. From their name people said they were Spare tires of inferior manufacture and only used in an emergency. They had thin faces and buck teeth and high voices. Gaeglers disliked them but they had been reared in the same street as himself and Gaeglers would hate anybody to think he was a snob. They worked occasionally and on the side they were snatchers and snitchers, that is they would steal little things that nobody would make a fuss about, like linen sheets off a clothes line, or even, some unkind people said, babies' rattlers out of prams, and if they saw anybody else doing an honest bit of stealing they would burn the leather of their shoes running to tell the authorities about it. As you see, not pleasant types at all; but Gaeglers was feeling charitable, so he saluted them.

"Hello, Twotees," he said pleasantly, "what has you pair out here? Stealing milk from country cows?"

They giggled in their high voices.

"You're a laugh, Gaeglers," said Twotee Tee. "It was such a nice evening that we had to come for a walk."

Gaeglers was horrified to think that the same God of them all could have inspired such characters with the same thought that had been put into his own head.

"I hope it keeps fine for you," he said, hoping they would pass on. But they didn't. They were determined to walk with him. Worse, they started gabbing all the stuff about Do you remember. When they were all young. Gaeglers told himself, thinking back, that he had nothing to reproach himself with over his youth, but the two beside him should have tried their best to forget their snivelling young days, which as far as he could remember were nothing but a series of whining and pinching and petty larceny and playing horrible tricks on old itinerants or old country people who couldn't answer back or defend themselves. Mean kids they were who always seemed to be saved from justice by the hand of the devil, people said. Exasperating. Gaeglers thought that it was only the fact that God allowed things like snakes and serpents and lizards and swamps and nauseating things that could account at all for the creation and existence of the Twotees.

So they giggled and gaggled and hissed and caught his arm to emphasise a remembrance, and Gaeglers thought there was a bit of a saint in him the way he put up with them. And then they heard the voice of the young girl screaming.

It came from down near the sea. There was a fall of about four feet from the promenade to the stones of the shore. Gaeglers didn't wait. He jumped and ran towards the sound of the screaming. As he came near the water he could see two figures that appeared to be struggling. He took the pencil torch from his pocket and depressed the switch. He was proud of this torch. It was powerful. It shone on the two. One was a very young girl. He would put her age at sixteen. She looked into the light of the torch with terrified eyes. She was being held by two sinewy hands with black hair on the backs of them. Gaeglers didn't delay. He reached forward and hit the face of the man with the back of his hand. He staggered, releasing the girl. Gaeglers looked at her. Calm now. Cheap summer dress. Highheeled shoes, lipstick amateurishly applied. Blue on her eyes. A silly kid that had got hold of her sister's make-up box.

"Go home out of that, you silly little bitch," he said to her. "Have you no sense!"

Maybe she expected kindness from him, or to be soothed. Her mouth was open. She was holding the torn front of her dress with one hand, a child's hand. "Go on home out of that when I tell you," he shouted, "or I'll give you something!"

She looked at him once, and then she turned and walked towards the promenade, stumbling on the rounded stones.

He shone the light back on the man. He didn't know him. He would be a stranger. Not that one of the locals wouldn't fiddle a girl in a dark corner, but not a daft young dilly like that picked up in the fun fair, a stupid daft child with no sense.

He had no hat, the man. He was bald and his bald head and face were very brown from the sun. He wore light clothes and a silk tie and his stomach protruded. He had very thin lips and hooded eyes. Gaeglers didn't like the look of his face at all.

Then matters were taken out of his hands.

The Twotees came from behind him. Then went one each side of the man and held his arms and started to beat him with their open hands.

"A fiddler," said Twotee Tee. Slap.

"A conch," said Twotee To. Slap.

Gaeglers pulled them away and pushed them from the man. He was rubbing his face with his hand.

"Stop that," said Gaeglers. Like two cuddies they were biting viciously at a battle-defeated dog.

"What's the idea?" he asked the man. "Would you do a thing like that at home would you? Why do you come here to do a thing like that?" Gaeglers was really disgusted. He had a high opinion of women.

"Did nothing," the man said. He had a hoarse voice. He spoke well. Well educated anyhow. No noticeable accent. "Just brought the girl for a walk," he said. "Nothing wrong with that."

"Not if you were her father," said Gaeglers.

"We'll throw him into the sea," said Twotee Tee.

"That'll cool the dirty one off," said Twotee To.

"Take off your trousers," said Gaeglers.

"What!" the man ejaculated.

"Off with the trousers," said Gaeglers.

The Twotees laughed.

"Jay, that's it!" they said.

"Now look," the man said. "Can't we forget this?" He was reaching into his pocket for money.

"Off with the trousers," said Gaeglers.

"Maybe we ought to listen a bit more to him," said Tee.

"It mightn't have been his fault," said To.

"Off with the trousers," said Gaeglers.

There was silence. The man sensed that the voice of Gaeglers was implacable.

He loosened the belt of his trousers and let them fall. He raised a foot awkwardly and freed his leg from the trousers. He didn't look well in his shirt and his stomach and the striped short pants. He handed over the trousers.

"You'll pay for this," the man said.

Gaeglers took the trousers.

"You'll find them on the last seat of the promenade," he said. "You will only have to walk two miles to get to them. While you are trying to slink the two miles without people seeing you, you can reflect on your evil ways and be glad nothing worse is happening to you."

"You'll pay for this," the man said.

"Come on," said Gaeglers to the others, and he went back up and got on to the promenade.

"Jay, that was a good one," said Tee.

"Real hot," said To. "I wonder who was the one that was with him. Maybe we ought to date her."

They giggled.

Gaeglers paid no attention to them. He walked to the end of the promenade to the last seat. It was getting late. There was nobody there. He was about to throw the trousers under the seat when he felt the bulk in the hip pocket. He took out the bulk. It was a wallet. He opened it. There were notes in it. He counted them with the Twotees breathing on him. Twelve pounds. Other things and a card. The man's name was Ginter. It suited him. Gaeglers reflected that he had been on the side of justice. He had fought for the right. Now it was only just that he should be rewarded. What could the man do? Nothing. He would be too ashamed. He'd slink away in the night and write the money off to experience. "Here," said

Gaeglers, and he split the money and gave the Twotees six pounds. "Go home now and keep your mouths shut." He put back the money-empty wallet, threw the trousers under the seat and walked away.

He didn't realise how careless and foolish he had been until the police called for him and brought him down to the barracks and charged him with the stealing of twelve pounds with menaces. It took Gaeglers a long time to realise that he was in the hands of the police for the first time in his life and that he was about to receive the kiss of death.

He sat in the courtroom and he heard Ginter tell how while peacefully out walking for his health he had been accosted at a dark place by this man whom he now recognized, that he had been beaten and that when he came to his senses he was without his trousers. He was followed by the Twotees. They swore one after the other that when going peacefully for a walk they had seen Gaeglers, whom they knew well, taking something from a trousers and throwing the trousers under a seat. They had taken the trousers when he departed, wondered at it, and walked back along the promenade until they met this man without trousers creeping back by the wall. They had listened to his story, were very indignant at the treatment meted out to him and had been more than pleased to go to the police with their story. They were sorry that the good name of the town should be hurt by things like this. They were all for tourist travel, and they regretted that things like this might give the town a bad name and that the tourist trade would fall off.

Gaeglers was dumbfounded. In the end it was only the sense of humour he had that could come to his aid. He decided to take his medicine. He knew that Ginter was a bad man. He knew that a sixpenny bit would buy the Twotees. He now knew the family of the terrified girl. They were very decent, respectable people. They knew nothing at all about their daughter's adventure. He could name her and have her brought here. He didn't like the thought of that. He thought that would be a greater evil than his own case. He had no mother or father, kith or kin, and anyhow, he thought, it will be interesting to see how our jail system functions.

So he called no witnesses; had no solicitor to defend him. He went into the box, looked into the shrewd and puzzled eyes of the magistrate.

Said Gaeglers: "If I took some money from this man, I am guilty, sir. But I would like to say that the story of the Spares is a pack of lies. I would like to say that the major part of Ginter's story is a lie. That the Spares are weasels who have been bought so that they may perjure themselves to injure me; that there is nothing for you to do except find me guilty and pass sentence."

The magistrate said: "You have nothing more to say?"

"No, sir," said Gaeglers.

The magistrate said, "There is something here I don't understand."

A lot of good that did him.

He sentenced Gaeglers to six months.

Gaeglers saw the eyes of Ginter as he left. They were cold eyes, glinting. He had said, "You'll pay for this." Gaeglers would pay. He saw the Twotees. Now that it was over, their eyes were frightened. Gaeglers had thought that his reputation would have kept them on his side. But obviously money overcame their fear.

"I'll be seeing you, boys," he said as he passed. It gave him some satisfaction to see them swallowing their Adam's apples.

This is the story of why Gaeglers went to jail for the one and only time in his life. He learned lessons from it. It was all his fault. The first awful mistake he made was to put his trust in two withered reeds like the Twotees. Normally he would never have done it. Nothing would have happened if he hadn't gone for a walk. He discovered that he had a great weakness. He was sentimental. Any more when he felt himself becoming sentimental, he must run away. Also he must see to it on his return that the Twotees would suffer a little for their betrayal.

They suffered quite a bit before his return. Ginter's money didn't last long, and then they started to count off the days on the calendar. Gaeglers' friends (he had a lot of friends) didn't help them either. They were ostracized in society. That didn't hurt them much, because they were used to it, but occasionally they were stopped and told that Gaeglers had written to a friend and he hoped that they were enjoying life – the Twotees, that is – because they hadn't much longer left. If their hair didn't turn grey before Gaeglers' release it was because they were too stupid, but not insensitive.

Gaeglers was released after four months and two weeks. He was very popular in that jail. Believe me. If ever you go there and enquire about him this will be confirmed. The prisoners were sorry to see him go, and so was the staff. He certainly lightened the burden for them, and for a century or so to come they will date things before or after "the time Gaeglers was here."

On his release, the Twotees lived like rats. They only came out at night. They were more furtive than rats. They dodged and they twisted and they turned, but it was inevitable that one day Gaeglers should corner them. It was a real corner. They were between two houses and a wall, sucking the butts of cigarettes, when he loomed in front of them. There was no escape. He stood there tall, his legs spread, his hands crooked and a smile on his face. They were just petrified. He walked slowly towards them smiling, and they couldn't move. And he reached a hand for each of them and he caught a lapel of each jacket, and it took a superhuman effort on his part not to bash their two thin heads together until the half-ounce of brains they had came out through the cracks.

Instead he spoke to them, softly, kindly, and this at first seemed to terrify them even more.

"Boys," said Gaeglers, "let's be friends. Let's forgive and forget."

They couldn't believe their ears.

"Wh-what did you say?" Tee squeaked.

"Leave us alone," chimed To.

"Look," said Gaeglers, "I know it wasn't really the fault of you boys. The fellow tempted you, didn't he?"

"That's right, Gaeglers," said Tee in a burst. "He came after us. He gave us five pounds each. Honest, Gaeglers, we'd never have done it but we needed the money bad. The aunt wanted to go to hospital for an operation."

"That's right," said To, "her cries were pitiful."

My God, Gaeglers thought, what miserable liars they are!

"Listen," he said. "I'm really sorry for your aunt, and I hope she got over the operation."

"No," said Tee, "she died, and we had to spend the money on the funeral."

"That's right," said To, "easy come, easy go. Like that. The Lord took her."

"Ah, well," said Gaeglers. "That's very sad. I feel for you. Anyhow it was all a mistake, so tell you what, just to prove we are friends again why don't you come up tomorrow Sunday and have dinner in the digs with me. We'll talk the whole thing over. How about that, hah?"

"You're a gent, Gaeglers," said Tee. "A proper gent. I knew you'd take it like this. Didn't I tell To that you were a proper gent and that there was nothing to be afraid of?"

"That's right," said To, "Tee practically loves you, Gaeglers."

"Tomorrow so, at the digs," said Gaeglers. "Goodbye."

And he put his hands in his pockets and walked away from them, whistling cheerfully.

"Well, imagine that," said Tee.

"God is good," said To, and both of them felt that they had been freed from sudden death.

They knocked tentatively on the door of Gaeglers' digs the next day in good time. They were very cleaned up and still a little apprehensive, unbelieving. But Gaeglers himself came to the door and greeted them expansively and welcomed them in and brought them into the rarely used parlour, where there was a spotless white cloth and gleaming cutlery on the table. He chatted with them amiably and said: "You know I should be grateful to you boys for sending me to jail. I had a wonderful time there." And he entertained them with a gay account of his incarceration, which was mostly true, and they laughed with him, mostly in joyful relief. Then he said when he heard the lady outside calling: "Well, it's all ready. We are having duck today. The woman is a great hand at duck. We'll have the soup first." And he went out himself and brought it in. Three plates of soup he set there, and they gobbled it with their spoons, but he was talking so much that he only toyed with his and didn't touch it. You'd think the two hadn't a meal for ten years the way they got rid of the soup. They all but licked the plates. Then Gaeglers went out of the room, and when he came back he was carrying a black pot with no lid on it, and there was steam rising from it.

"Did you like the soup, boys?" he asked.

"Jay, it was smashin' soup," they said.

"Well, I'm glad," said Gaeglers putting his hand in the pot. "Because it was good soup. See what it was made of." And in front of their paling eyes he reached into the pot and pulled out the body of a dead cat and held it wet and dangling in front of them.

He really dangled it. With great interest he watched the way the green look started to come into their faces. Green like the colour of the sea on a summer day or better still an autumn day, and he kept dangling it until Tee said, "Oh, no! Oh, no!"

and his hand went up to his mouth and he ran for the door. Gaeglers opened the door for them and he also opened the front door for them and rubbed them with the dead cat as they went out and watched them for a while as they vomited their guts out on the pavement. Then he closed the door on them and put the cat back in the pot and dumped both out in the back yard, and came back to the dining room and placidly started to spoon his own plate of soup.

That's the cream of the joke, Gaeglers thought. It's real duck soup, and nice duck soup, but nothing could possibly persuade them to the contrary. Not now.

The Fair Lady

———◦———

DOWN OUR PLACE where we live by the sea there is a very great stretch of sand between our mainland and an island that is four miles from us. The sand is between the island and the mainland. The tide covers it when it comes in but not very deeply. It is very firm sand. It's nearly the same walking on it as walking on a tarred road, it is so firm, and that is the reason why every year we hold the races on it. Entries for our races come from all over the province, but it is very rarely that a foreign horse walks away with the main prize. We consider that it would be totally unfair for a foreign horse to win the main prize, and so we, the members of the committee (who handicap the horses), take good care that an honest local man with his horse wins the prize. We have also a special race for outsiders and whoever likes can win that one as long as the main race, the Gold Cup, remains at home. Everyone who comes has a very good time since we are a hospitable people, and they are always longing for next year so that they may come back to us. We know that on the outside all horse racing is crooked. Even those very big races are crooked, as we read sometimes in the papers. Fellows switching horses and doing odd tricks to bookies over bets and things, giving horses dope and drugs and the devil knows what. We are well aware of all this, so our races are always very clean. The only complaint is the one we get from foreigners, that some of the winners are predictable; but then foreigners always complain even when things are perfect.

I have always complete trust in our races and our committee, all good honest local men, businessmen, farmers, etc., and if they are a bit crooked in their own business, who isn't, but they have always been decent and upright as far as the local races go, and I swear on my oath that the only time I have known any unfairness was last year over the case of the Fair Lady, and that is why I am writing this down in the books – I am the Secretary and Treasurer (Hon.).

This business would never have cropped up at all if our Hon. Chairman hadn't gone and bought a pony. He happened to be at the fair in the big town selling cattle and saw this black pony and nothing on God's earth would do him but to buy the pony and bring it home and start training it for the big Gold Cup race. Nobody knew why he did it. I doubt if he even knew himself. You'd think that being on the Committee would have been enough for him, but no, he has to buy this black pony. He was just bitten by the bug, that was all, so the first we know of it he is down on the sands when the tide is out and his youngest son is up on the pony's back chasing hell out of the beast up and down.

Naturally we accost him and ask him what's up. He has a great light in his eye. "You are looking," he says, "at this year's winner of the Gold Cup." We say: "Look, we don't know what's got into you, but don't you know better than anyone else that Bogeen's Fair Lady is bound to win the race because nothing like her has been seen around here for eight years." She is a lovely little mare belonging to Bogeen. He is a very popular man, Bogeen. He is a small weeshie little fellow, who has a small little wife and four of the smallest children you ever saw in your life. He always rides Fair Lady himself. He looks like a boy up on the pony's back and anybody can see that in his small children he is rearing up a generation of jockeys; but they won't always have a Fair Lady. Turbot, who is the local fish merchant, and myself point out all this to the Hon. Chairman, but he is very smug and he says: "This black pony has the beating of Fair Lady in every hoof of him and if anybody thinks any different they are entitled to their opinions and I am giving two to one."

"I'll take ten pounds' worth of that," said Turbot, very fast, and what could I do then but say, "I'll take another ten on it." It wasn't strictly legal for us to do this because there is a rule that says members of the committee must not bet money on the races, but then what is legal, after all. We parted from the Hon. Chair., and Turbot and I walked away and Turbot is rubbing his hands. "My God, Hon. Sec.," he says, "we will never earn money easier than that. I have been watching the black pony and even though he is fast, Bogeen's Fair Lady won't even have to work up a sweat to leave him standing." "That's true," I said, "but somehow, knowing the Hon. Chair. as I do, I am now sorry I was so fast opening my big mouth. Fair Lady will have to be handicapped after all because she won last year. The black will have to get a five-yard start on her. What about that?" "It doesn't matter," Turbot said. "If he got twenty yards on her, he still wouldn't do it. The Fair Lady will leave him cold."

I didn't feel easy in my mind all the same. I know the Hon. Chairman. He is a very nice fellow, but he is successful in business and he didn't become a success throwing ten-pound notes all over the place. But in the rush and bustle of all the preparations for the race, writing letters and begging for funds, etc., I was very busy and the whole thing slipped out of my head until the eve of the races when Turbot came over to my place of business in an agitated condition. "You must come with me fast," he said. "I have received a terrible report that Bogeen has the Fair Lady out under a cart and is drawing turf home from the bog with her." I said: "No! No! Not the day before the race. I wouldn't believe that of Bogeen. Why, Bogeen practically puts Fair Lady into his own bed for a week before the race. Just gentle runs upon the sand, etc." Turbot says: "Well, he's not, and let's go and see or there will be a great scandal about the whole affair."

Bogeen lived quite a way from the rest of us. Up a road that climbed the height of a steep hill behind the lake. We were nearly tired out ourself when we got to his house and we were riding in Turbot's van. Mrs Bogeen looked at us with sad sort of eyes when we asked her about her husband. Her eyes were red, like she was crying, and I thought that this sight was very sinister, and I was practically bidding goodbye to my ten pounds. We walked the rest of the way and it was heavy going. About two miles up the road we see Bogeen walking by Fair Lady's head and she hauling and dragging at a cart full of heavy stone-turf.

We stop him indignantly.

"Why, Bogeen," Turbot says, "I am horrified. I am truly horrified."

Bogeen's head was down. The Fair Lady was glad of the rest. Anybody could see that. She was a beautiful pony – you know the colour, sort of reddish brown all over her body and her mane and tail coloured platinum. Bogeen was rubbing her nose with his small hand, and she was nuzzling into his palm. This pony loved Bogeen, as everybody knew and also everybody knew that he was soft about the pony.

"I never would have believed it," said Turbot. "Honest, Bogeen, a man like you to do that to a delicate racing pony. What has come over you? What spirit of unwonted cruelty has moved you to such a terrible deed?" I could see that Turbot was also worried about his ten pounds.

Bogeen left his pony and walked to a hillock at the side of the road and sat down on it. Then he took off his cap and he rubbed it all over his face. He put the cap back on and then he spoke.

"I am a miserable man," said Bogeen. "I never thought I'd see the day, but what could I do? I could do nothing else."

"Why, man, why, tell us why?" Turbot insisted.

"Well," said Bogeen, "you know the Hon. Chairman bought a black stallion pony."

"Yes," said Turbot.

"Well, there you are," said Bogeen. "The Hon. Chairman came to me. You know he owns the shop and you know that he gives the lot of us credit. I still owe him for last year's artificial manure and many other sundries, which I always pay for later on when the harvest is in and home. You know that?"

"I think I do," said Turbot. I joined Bogeen at the side of the road and prepared to whistle goodbye to my money.

"Also," said Bogeen, "I rent three acres of conacre from him. You know that. So when he comes to me and says that it would be a pity if his pony didn't win the Gold Cup, what can I do? I said I would withdraw Fair Lady, but he said this mightn't look nice, so it would be better if I gave her lots of work to do for a few days before so that she might not be in good fettle, that nothing thereafter would be changed."

"May God forgive the crafty son-of-a-bitch," said Turbot joining us. After that Turbot didn't ask God to forgive the Hon. Chairman. He cursed him very severely in two languages.

"I wouldn't mind, in a way," said Bogeen, "but she knows. As true as you are there, she knows. I swear an oath, I'm afraid to look her in the two eyes, I'm so ashamed, so I am. Fair Lady might forgive me but I will never forgive myself, even if I live to be a hundred, but what could I do? I have a wife and four children."

Turbot was foaming at the mouth. He got up and he kicked stones around the road. Then he stood in front and he looked at the drooping Lady.

"Bogeen," he said, "you have really worked her hard, haven't you?"

"She's eager," said Bogeen. "That's her trouble. She is too eager. You can't stop her once she starts."

"Bogeen," said Turbot, "how good really is this pony?"

Bogeen said: "She is the best pony in the whole world." He said it simply.

"Listen," said Turbot. "Are you willing to place your whole future on the back of that pony?"

"How?" Bogeen asked.

"We are on a good thing," said Turbot. "Everybody now knows that the black pony is fixed to win the Gold Cup. Suppose we gather all the money we can lay our hands on, we'll get odds at four to one. This is a chance for one of the greatest coups in the history of the turf. Let us work all the rest of the day and all the night and morning on Fair Lady. Let us make her win this race against all the odds and we will have enough out of it to make the Hon. Chairman go and take a running jump at himself. You can clear your debts with him and rent different conacre next year. How about it?"

"Oh, how I wish it!" said Bogeen. "But look at her. I have killed her. I have taken everything out of her. She just hasn't anything left in her."

"We'll see," said Turbot. "Nobody can do a thing like that to me. The dirty twister. Imagine doing a thing like that. She'll win this race tomorrow dammit, if I have to run in myself and carry her on my back."

He started to untackle the Fair Lady.

Now what happened after that is history. We walked the Fair Lady down below to her stable and Turbot and Bogeen took off their coats and they started to rub her all over with liniment, and then I took the van and went down to the place below and I bought oats and whiskey, good stuff, ten years old. And I went back surreptitiously with this, and the oats were heated and some of the whiskey was given to the Fair Lady to drink so that she became a bit squiffy and lay down, and some of the whiskey was applied externally to the muscles and the places in her that needed it most. And then she was roused and gently walked and I went off below.

I saw the Hon. Chair. He was looking very cheerful. I put on an air of innocence as if I was the only one in the whole world who didn't know that the race was all fixed. He said to me: "What about your ten quid, Joe, will you pay up now or wait until tomorrow?" I said: "You poor sucker. Bogeen will have that pony like a sheet of lightning by tomorrow. Fair Lady will pass your black pony running backwards." From this conversation he knew that I didn't know what everybody else knew, and he said, "If you believe that, back your opinion," and I pretended to be very excited and before we knew where we were in front of witnesses, I had placed a hundred pounds with him at four to one. Then I went home and prayed that Fair Lady wouldn't send us all into bankruptcy and that if Turbot had led me astray that he might be smitten by lightning.

The day dawned very beautiful. Oh, a lovely day. Clear blue sky with the sun shining on the sands. The stalls were up with colourful covers on them and everybody was there from all over. Also the bookies were there – the only two who ever came. They were shocking cautious because they didn't trust many people and in order to win a pound or two you'd want to put down a thousand. The two early races were run off and the favourites won, and then we were up on the Gold Cup and there was the Hon. Chairman, the bastard, beaming and smiling as if he was honest and his black pony glistening in the sun and along comes Fair Lady and her coat wasn't glistening. She looked very depressed and her coat very dry. That was because, Turbot said, they had worked all night on her and then had rubbed dust all over her and had brushed the dust backwards into her. Bogeen up on her back held her head down as if she was in the middle of a depression coming from Iceland, and everybody who came and looked at her nodded their heads and hummed and hawed and winked and tried to get a bob or two on the black. Nobody was betting on Fair

Lady except myself, and I looking as innocent as possible and praying like mad; but we got on another fifty pounds with local men at six to one, and I thought, Well, if this doesn't come off we will have to leave the country.

Well, I have to hand it to Fair Lady. There was never anything like her since our races began. By God, it was really wonderful. She went over that sand and you'd think her belly was touching it. She almost didn't win of course – how could she after what had happened? But she won by her head, by her forehead. There was no doubt about it. I had to admire the way Bogeen and Turbot had worked over Fair Lady.

I enjoyed the face of the Hon. Chairman. It was worth three years in jail to see the face of the Hon. Chairman.

The only trouble was that it was very hard on Fair Lady. Afterwards when I went to Bogeen with the substantial amount that was coming to him I couldn't give it to him. I had to give it to Mrs Bogeen. Because the pony was out in the stable lying in the straw and Bogeen was hunched over her crying his eyes out.

But it was all marvellous. It was really marvellous the way Turbot and myself got over the Hon. Chairman. He was a good sport. He acknowledged the whole thing afterwards when we agreed that next year his black pony would win the Gold Cup (we agreed on this when we heard the Fair Lady was dead), and that's what we are getting ready for now, and mind you he is a good pony this black. The trouble is that there is absolutely no opposition to him and you can't get a price on him, but anyhow now it's recorded the tale of that year's Gold Cup. We are hoping that Bogeen will get over the loss of his pony. After all a pony is just a pony and there are thousands of them around and it is very foolish of Bogeen to be grieving like this over what was after all only an animal, and sort of blaming Turbot and myself for doing him a real favour, and we hope that he doesn't really mean it when he swears that he will never go up on the back of a pony again. With Bogeen out of it the races don't seem to be as good as they were somehow. But that's human nature. He will come around. After all, our races are important.

The Lady and the Tom

————————◇————————

I F YOU LEFT the main tarred road that passed through
the village, winding its way back towards the tall mountains,
and turned off on the flint road that meandered by the
lake, twisting and winding, taking its shape from the contour
of the hard hills it was skirting, and if you walked along this
road for three or four miles, you would inevitably meet her.

It is peculiar country. Around you on the shore of the lake
and bordering the road it is fertile, and in parts tropical, with
acres of rearing forest trees, spruce and larch and silver fir
dominating them; fuchsia hedges heavy with the red suckers
beloved of the bees, impenetrable clumps of briar and tall
thorn bushes almost strangled with wild woodbine tendrils or
wound thickly with ivy and dying in its embrace. And if you
climbed the hills you would climb into almost eternal loneliness, bracken and furze giving way to rough sedge and the
wet boglands.

So it is odd to see Miss Vincent walking on this road.

You look around to see if there is a long black car, old and
well looked after, with a chauffeur in uniform smoking a cigarette while he awaits her return. Because that is the thought
that she puts into your head. She is a tall lady and she is bent
a little. Her hair is grey, almost white, and sometimes she
wears a big round pot-hat decorated with artificial cherries.
But she wears this only on the warm days. Other days she has
a neat umbrella, or in a gesture to conform with modern life
she will be wearing a head-scarf. It is modest in colour and
always tones with the light grey knitted suits she wears. Her

stockings will be woollen, winter and summer, and her black shoes with the medium heel are always shining. She uses a slender blackthorn stick to help her. It is her only companion. A gold wedding ring is glinting on her right hand, but if you get close enough you will see that it is well worn and it belonged to her dear dead mother.

The people around are used to queer people.

The oddest individuals come to the hotels in the small fishing village to capture the trout and salmon in the lake in the seasons when they are plentiful and biting freely. They are mainly loud-mouthed people who dress in the most peculiar clothes imaginable. They have big swooshing cars or hunting brakes. They have plenty of money and they come and go so that the people become as used to them as they do to the swallows and the wild geese. They tell you the seasons of the year.

But Miss Vincent was different.

She came and when she should have gone away people saw that she was still there, so she aroused curiosity.

There was a sort of old fishing hut down by the lake, with an atrocious road going into it, that was a welter of mud in the winter. It had just two rooms. It wasn't ever meant to be anything but a casual place where males would pig it out for a few weeks of the fishing season, and the owner was startled when he was asked if he would sell it. Before he got time to think he sold it for a hundred pounds and cursed himself afterwards because he could have got more.

Miss Vincent bought it. For exactly one hundred and fifty pounds extra she got necessary repairs done to the iron roof, the inside boarded neatly to keep out the draughts, and a little hand pump that brought water up to a cistern that would supply the water for sanitation and washing and all the rest of it.

It took a very small van to bring her stuff, people noticed. It was unloaded and put into the house in about half an hour, although the driver of the van grumbled terribly in a Dublin accent about how was he going to get the van in and out of that bit of dirt track, that was probably laid down by the Milesians. One or two men helped him carry in the bits and pieces because they wanted to report what sort she was since she would be living with them for a time. The stuff, they reported, was very old-fashioned but most substantial, and she was a nice little woman for an Englishwoman, speaking in the clipped English way; but she was pleasant to them and thanked them nicely for their help and she appeared to be all right.

She didn't get many letters, so it was some time before the postman could report how she was settling in. When he did have to go down there, it was well on in the autumn and the cold winds were beginning to come sliding over the hills, and the lake had the cold repelling look on it that would make you shiver at the thought of your body being immersed in it, even in a good cause. She was snug, the postman reported at the Cross House. This was up the bend of the road about half a mile away from the turn down to Miss Vincent's. It was an ordinary thatched cottage that wasn't thatched now but was roofed with corrugated iron and was owned by a man called Dumper Delaney. Dumper was a bachelor, by choice. Nobody knew his age. He could have been fifty or he could have been ninety, but he was probably sixty. He still had thick black hair that he rarely combed. He was big and inclined to be fat and he ran a bit of a shop in the place, where he sold tea and sugar and tobacco and odds and ends to save people from having to walk the long way to the village for their sheer necessities. He didn't make much money, just enough to keep him going, and the kids had him robbed because he was always giving them a free handful of sweets from the tin, so how the hell could he make a profit? He was happy, and his house was a meeting place, coming or going, morning, noon or night. He always had a big fire blazing in the open hearth, and it was a great place in the winter to steam wet clothes dry or to shake the snow off yourself. He was avidly interested in everybody within an area of four miles all around. He knew their names and birthdays and peculiarities and diseases and when they came and where they went and when they would be coming home. But he was charitable. Sometimes he was so charitable that he would madden you. He was always the man with the good word in his mouth.

He felt sorry for Miss Vincent when the winter came in.

"I wonder is she lonely down there?" he asked the postman.

"Why would she?" the postman asked. "Isn't she English? None of the English that come here is ever lonely. They have themselves and they are pleased with their own company."

"No," said Dumper. "After all, the poor old bitch is a human being. It's a lonely spot down there in the winter with the wind skitin' off the lake."

The postman had a letter for her in November.

The lane down to her place was a sea of mud now. He couldn't ride a bicycle down there, so he cursed like hell trying to walk on the tips of stones protruding out of the mud, and slipping off them and going ankle-deep and thinking what a good job it was that rubber boots were invented.

He was surprised how neat she had the place in front of the small tin hut. The hut was gleaming too with red iron oxide paint. She had flower beds laid and a small patch of a lawn, and the stones around it were whitewashed. The panes of glass were gleaming bluely and there were bits of nice-coloured chintz curtains behind them. She had a brass knocker on the door and it was glinting. He knocked.

He was a phlegmatic man but he was surprised out of it by the effusive way she welcomed him. Her eyes widened and there was a flush on her pale cheeks.

"I'm pleased to see you," she said. "A letter for me? How nice! Won't you come in and sit down for a moment? It's a cold day. There is a good fire."

He was so surprised that he went in. He didn't go in everywhere. How could he? If he went in everywhere he'd never be done.

It was a very neat sparkling room the way she had it. A mahogany table behind with four chairs around it, and near the fire two comfortable armchairs and doodahs on a sideboard and small delicate sort of pictures on the walls. Very snug, he told them later. She insisted on making tea and offering him a cup. They were tiny teacups, soft to the touch like velvet, he reported, but they would be lost in your hand and if your wife offered you one of them for your breakfast tea you'd go proper mad and probably hit her. He felt awkward in there. He felt very big, like he was a bullock. You should ha' seen me, he said, juggling with them thimble cups and atin' a biscuit. But he was a shrewd enough man and he knew that Miss Vincent was lonely. And he felt sorry for her. Very sorry.

"You have such a long way to travel," she chattered. "It is so cold and wet and damp."

"You get used to it," he told her.

He stayed about fifteen minutes.

Miss Vincent was sorry when he had gone.

She sat and opened her letter. It was from an old friend back home. It seemed so far away back home. The cottages with the mullioned windows and the decorative thatch and the red board outside the inn and the small grey church with the Norman tower and the ducks on the grey green. Tears came into her eyes, but she wiped them away. The letter from the friend was nothing. She tore it up. She thought how pleased she had been to see the postman. She thought of back home. She tried in vain to see the postman back home coming into the living room and sitting down having a cup of tea with dear Papa. Papa with his smoking jacket and his red face and his utter and absolute and all-enveloping selfishness. If it wasn't for dear Papa, she would be married now. There was the young man. There was the other young man. But Papa was so overpowering, and when Mamma died he required so much attention. She should have deserted him, but then she hadn't had the courage. She had the courage to do this about coming to live here, but that was the courage of necessity. It was very nice. It was very nice, but it was a teeny bit lonely. It took a long time to get used to the moaning of the wind across the lake and to hear the lonely call of birds in the nighttime, the occasional reverberation of a shotgun. That's morbid, she thought and cleaned up the cups.

"The poor bitch," said Dumper. "She mustn't have a sinner in the world. She showed no interest in the letter at all."

"Not a pick," said the postman.

"She must be awful lonely," said Dumper.

"She should have got herself a man," said the postman.

"She should have got herself an animal," said Dumper, taking a black kitten from his neck. Dumper had millions of black kittens. They were everywhere, and white ones and grey ones and multicoloured ones.

He was pleased one day she came into his shop. It was a cold frosty day in January. She wanted sugar and tea. The van from the village had failed to call on account of the heavy freezing. He made her sit at the fire on a stool. She took off her gloves and stretched her hands. They were small, fine-boned hands, he saw. One of the kittens jumped upon her lap, a small jet-black fellow. She jumped up with a scream. She had her hand to her heart.

"Forgive me," she said. "I don't like cats. He startled me."

"Why don't you like cats?" Dumper asked, taking up the black fellow and stroking him.

She thought, Why don't I like cats?

"My Papa didn't like cats, Mr Delaney," she said. "He would never have one in the house." That's why I don't like cats, she thought with wonder, because Papa didn't like cats.

"Feel the fur of that one," said Dumper holding him out. "He's a little beauty."

It took her some time, but then she reached a hand and gently rubbed the kitten's fur. The kitten purred. He stretched to her.

"Go on," said Dumper, "take ahold of him."

She did so, tentatively. The kitten burrowed in her arms and rubbed his small head luxuriously against her coat. His body was warm. She could feel the warmth of it through her clothes.

"He's a nice little kitten," said Miss Vincent.

"Why don't you take him home with you?" Dumper asked.

"Oh, no, I couldn't," she protested.

"Why couldn't you?" Dumper probed.

"Because ..." she started. Then she thought. Then she spoke. "Why, there's no reason at all, why I shouldn't," she said. "But will you be lonely for him?"

Dumper laughed.

"I have millions of them," said Dumper. He liked the way there was a shine in her eyes. "He's a clean cat."

She brought him home. She did what Dumper said and she never had to clean up after him. She talked to him. It felt good to have him in the lonely nice little house. She felt well. The winter howled itself away, and before she knew it the spring was in. The kitten was big. She called him Surrey. He went with her everywhere. It was quite a sight to see Miss Vincent walking the road with the black kitten walking with her. Quite a sight. It made people smile in a pleased sort of way.

Then he was gone.

Just gone. He just went away. It was only then she realised how much the kitten had meant to her. She knew he was killed, by a badger or a dog or by a careless car. She waited for three days and then she went to ask about.

Dumper was red in the face, but he couldn't come straight out with it. He's a tom and he's on the tiles. How could you say that to a nice old lady who probably still believed that men were born out of heads of cabbage. He tried to reassure her. So did everybody else. She asked at every house along the road. They were all very kind and some of them smiled when she had gone. Some of them laughed out loud, but it was kind laughter. There was nobody could come flat out with it, that the tom was on the tiles.

Miss Vincent thought her little house was very bleak. Even though the waters of the lake were blue and sometimes the sun shone and the daffodils were sending shoots from below. Even all that. I feel worse, she thought, than when my Papa died.

Dumper brought back the cat. He had found him.

She was overjoyed.

For a time.

"Keep him at home for a while," Dumper said.

The cat didn't know her. His fur was up. He walked stiff-legged about the room, trying to go again. If she petted him, he didn't respond. He just looked at her with sort of wild eyes.

She felt very lonely. She cried, as he looked at her as if he had never seen her before.

"Even the animals," Miss Vincent said aloud, "even the animals."

In three days he responded to her. He purred to her petting and he walked at her heels. But somehow, Miss Vincent could never feel the same again about him. He will go again, she thought, like all the others.

She would have been despondent only for one thing.

When she walked the road people stopped her to ask about the cat.

"You got him back, thank God," they said in cheerful tones. "And isn't that grand." Lots of people. She got to know their names. She got to know their faces. They smiled at her and sometimes they told her things. And many days when she would be lonely below, a woman would come down with a basket and she would say: "Here is a young chicken, Miss Vincent, that got run over by a wheel and I plucked it and cleaned it, and wouldn't it be nice for your dinner?" Or a woman would come with a basket and a few eggs nestling in a cloth, or a man like Dumper heaving his great weight over the rough lane with a bag of potatoes or a few vegetables. Other things like that.

So when the next winter came and the spring and when Surrey went away again, Miss Vincent cried again, but she didn't cry because she was lonely.

This time she cried because she was happy.

The Atheist

H E WAS A pale and sickly boy. The fact was that it was regarded as a miracle he had survived into his seventh year. His mother said it was prayer alone that had made him live. He was a seventh son. His six brothers were tall and healthy and lusty, and their instinct was, like animals, to despise the weakling in the flock. His mother adored him. She would have given all the other six for him. His father was tall and black and a good worker. He felt bewildered when he looked at his seventh son. He felt that little Joe was a sort of reflection on him. But he was kind to him.

In the country district where they lived on a tidy farm that fed and clothed them, men who died at the age of ninety were thought of as being taken in the prime of life. They told the story of the mother and father who came back from the funeral of their son and sat over the fire sorrowing. The son had died at the age of seventy-two. The husband speaks. He says: Oh, Maggie, I told you when he was born that we would never rear him.

In a long-lived healthy place like this the little boy was an anomaly. He was a freak. The hard winters should have killed him off long ago. He seemed to be holding on to life with the greatness of his eyes. His eyes looked very big because his face and body were so emaciated. He coughed a terrible lot in the winter. It was his tubes, they said. They said it would have been better if God had taken him long ago. He will never age, they said. His mother thought he was a little saint, because suffering had laid a mark of patience on him. She never remembered him crying. He seemed to be intelligent beyond his years. He withstood unkindness and jeers from his healthy brethren as if it was part of living, so that teasing him lost its sting.

One day he wandered away from his own place.

Down the flint road he went on his thin legs. It was summertime and the sun was shining. He had never been that far afield before, but his mother was the only one at home. All the rest were in the hayfield. The road ran down a hill and wound around until it became a crossroads. He went left here on a worse road that went into a valley between two hills and then rose up, carving its way ever upwards beside a river that ran in pools and jagged rocks that it had indecently exposed from the flanks of the hill.

It took him quite a time. He sat down often on the grassy verges and he played with the small stones, or he scuffed his bare toes in the dust, making little mounds of it and blowing the mounds away. On each side of the road the hillsides stretched away deep in heather and wet boggy places that never dried. Small mountain sheep sometimes ran away from the road in front of him. Up and up he went unnoticing and he topped the hill and went down on the other side and then wandered off into a small road bordered by fuchsia hedges that had gained a hold in that bleak place. The ground was damp under his feet, and then he stood petrified as the huge dog came bounding from in front of him and stood there snarling and growling menacingly. The little boy felt cold things in his back. The dog showed no mercy. He was a very wicked dog. He was advancing snarling when the voice stopped him.

The man was much bigger than the dog. He was nearly as frightening. He seemed to be as hairy. The dog was brown and black and the man seemed to be the same. His clothes were brown and black and his face was brown and black with a close-trimmed beard on him. He cuffed the dog.

"Be quiet," he said to the dog.

He looked at the boy. The boy didn't feel any fear of the man. The man saw a pitifully thin body with matchstick legs, and a head that seemed very big because the brown hair wanted to be cut, and a thin, thin face under terrible big eyes. If the man felt anything in his heart, it didn't show in his eyes.

"Hello," he said. "The dog won't bite you. He only barks. Come and put your hand on him."

The boy looked at him and then advanced obediently. He stretched a skinny hand and laid it on the dog's head. The dog growled, and struggled a bit under the strong hand that held the fur on his neck. Then he submitted. The man noticed that the dog and the boy were the same height.

"Who are you?" the man asked.

"I'm Joe," the boy said.

"Who are you of?" the man asked.

The boy pointed back the way he had come. "From there," he said.

"Does your mother know you walked?"

Joe considered this. "I don't think so. She mebbe didn't see me."

"That's bad," said the man. "Come up, and we'll consider."

He reached his thick hand out and the boy put his own confidently into it. The man thought it was like feeling the claw of a chicken, the hand was so thin.

Around the bend, his house was. Joe thought it was only half as big as his mother's house. There was a fire in there. The man put him sitting on a low stool in front of the fire.

"You'll drink milk," the man said, and put a mug of it on the hob in front of him. Joe drank some of the milk. He had to use his two hands to raise the heavy mug to his face. He ate a bit of bread and butter too, but the man saw that he was only picking at it.

"If you're right now," the man said, "we'll take you home."

They walked down the road together. The man had to slow his pace. When they were halfway to the cross Joe had a fit of coughing. He sat down on the road to cough and held his hand to his chest. It didn't last long. The man just stood there looking down at him, clenching his hands. When the coughing was over he bent down and raised Joe into his arms and walked ahead with him. "See that fella, Joe? That's a hawk. Watch him swinging on the air. Now he'll dive. After a bird he is. That thing? That's a dirty oul grey crow. Grey crows is no damn good, Joe. In the snow on the hills when the sheep are bogged, they swoop and pluck out their eyes. Isn't that terrible? And they are bad on the lambs too."

Joe thought it was nice riding on the big man's arms. He could see miles down into the valleys where the lakes were and the houses. He was like a bird but not an oul grey crow.

When they neared his own place he saw his mother at the gate. She came running. She was very anxious. She took him from the man. There were tears in her eyes.

"Where were you? Where were you?" she cried. "I thought you were dead on me. I thought you were dead on me indeed."

"He went wandering, ma'am," the man said. "I found him up outside my place."

"But that's miles," she exclaimed. "But that's miles and miles. Oh, Joe!"

"He's a stout man," the man said. "Aren't you, Joe? Goodbye now." He held out his hand.

Joe reached out his own. "Goodbye," he said. "Can I see the dog again?"

The man looked at his mother. She was avoiding his eyes.

"We'll see, Joe," he said, and then he turned on his heel and went away.

She fussed over him terribly.

When his father and brothers came home, she told them all.

"What!" said the father. "Oul Peter. He shouldn't have gone near him. That oul atheist. Keep away from him, do you hear? That's a bad man, that oul Peter. No respect for church or chapel and eatin' meat on Fridays. You keep away from oul Peter, you hear."

It passed over Joe's head. Joe had had an adventure. He had been out in the world. He thought of the dog and the man and the grey crows.

"It did him good," his mother said. "He had a bit of colour in him. Maybe I keep him too close."

"It's no harm him being out a bit more," his father said. "As long as he keeps away from that oul atheist."

It happened that Joe wandered away many a day after that and he always or nearly always seemed to meet up with Peter and the bad dog. His mother lost her palpitations when he was absent. He always came home. She thought he was looking better. She thought maybe his eyes were getting smaller.

"What is an atheist?" Joe asked one day when he was sitting beside the dog and the two of them buried in the blooming purple heather.

There was a pause before Peter answered him.

"An atheist is a man, Joe, who doesn't believe in God," he said.

"Daddy said that you were a good man and then you went away and something happened to you out foreign and when you came back you were an atheist, and he says that's very bad; and I don't know but I think you're good and if you are an atheist couldn't I be one too?" He was breathless after that. It was a long speech.

Peter turned over on his belly to answer him. He took time over it.

"It's hard, Joe," he said. "Terrible things can happen to a man to change the whole course of his thinking. Great sorrow can happen to a man or great bitterness. That's one thing. Your father doesn't mean that. He means because nobody sees me in the little church below that I am a bad man. See, Joe, you look down there below, at the small town and the trees with the leaves falling off them and the lake and all the islands lying under the sun, and then over this side you look and you see the mountains going down and the sea out beyond, it blue and grey and stretching away until it meets the bottom of the clouds. You see all that?"

"I do," said Joe.

"Well, God is all that," said the grey man with the deeply lined face. "And when you see a lamb trying to walk or even an oul grey crow killing, or heather with colour in it, or the sun shining or the rain falling, God is in that, in the bark of a dog or the cry of a wild goose or the whistle of a flighting duck or in the eyes of a boy. God is in that, Joe. Do you understand that?"

"No," said Joe.

"You will," said Peter, "you will." But he was thinking that unless Joe got more meat on him or more colour in him, that he would meet God sooner than any other thing. And his heart was very heavy, because ever since he had allowed the big-eyed boy to break into his own terrible and self-inflicted loneliness, he had watched over him as you would a weak dog of a litter or a tottering lamb of a flock. He had become very fond of him and he knew this was wrong. He had never meant to become fond again of a single living thing.

It was unfortunate that Joe's father was at the lip of the road that day when he took him home.

He stood there watching them coming down the hill, the very big virile man with the bitter face and the changeling as he would one time have called him. Now he was the affliction of God. Anger rose in him at the sight. An unexplainable anger. The glaring contrast of opposites, and because Peter was a man nobody now understood, who went away from them and kept away as if they all had a disease.

"Where were you?" he asked angrily. "Your mother was worried about you. Where were you?" He didn't give him time to answer. He reached out a hard hand and hit him a cuff on the big head. The boy fell down. There was patient surprise in his eyes. He hadn't meant to hit him. He was a kind man. His action now drove him almost frantic with anger. "Never again up the hill!" he cried. "Never again up the hill, you hear!" He was glaring at Peter. He didn't know how close he had come to being battered himself.

Peter was white about the nostrils. His nails had bitten into his palms. He bent down and raised the boy to his feet. "Go on home, Joe," he said. "Goodbye." He watched him for a moment and then he turned and went away.

Joe's father was sweating with anger and mortification. His legs were trembling. He sat on a rock.

His wife came from the house. She was rubbing her hands on an apron. She was crying. "Why did you do it? Why did you do such a cruel thing? What's got into you? What's got into you at all?"

He got to his feet. "Leave me alone! Leave me alone for the love of Almighty God!" he shouted at her, and he strode wildly towards the turnip field.

So Joe didn't go up the hill again. Not until one day in January. He had been very sick before Christmas, and this time everybody said, He will surely die. But he didn't and they sent him to school. It was his first time at school. When they let them loose in the playground for the break Joe was terrified at the cruelty of the young children who were in the same class. It seemed to be instinctive with the lot of them to turn on him the minute they got out. Pinch and puck, and names. Joe couldn't understand it. He didn't cry, because he never did, but he didn't go back in again when the bell rang. His heart was beating very fast. He went away from the school and up the hill. He didn't go in to his mother. He went past his own gate and on up the hill. This was the first time he had gone up the hill since his father had told him not to. He was sure he would meet the dog and Peter. He was breathless when he came to the gaunt bare fuchsia bushes. He went up the lane and the door was locked and silent, so he turned and passed the house and went on into the mountains. It was very cold. People would never forget the cold of that January. No old person had ever heard of the like of it or seen it. The snow started to fall about three o'clock.

Joe wasn't missed until all his brothers came home from school. Where is Joe? Isn't he at home? No. Why didn't ye wait for him? Well, he wasn't there, we thought he had come home. His mother's heart sank. Her mouth was dry. Go and get your father. She ran down herself to the school. It was closed. She called at the teacher's. He didn't know anything. Little Joe hadn't come back after the break. He didn't know why. Little Joe, he told her, is a very intelligent child. I can do great things with him.

She was frantic now.

The father tried to calm her. She wouldn't be calmed. The dinner was neglected on the hob.

"He might be with that Peter," said the father.

She ran. The door was closed, the house was silent. Send him back to me, she prayed. Send him back to me now. The snow was falling quite thickly. The sky was the colour of copper. The father came with Peter. Peter had an ass with a bag of flour on its back and provisions. I was in town, he told them, getting things. He might have come here for all I know. I wasn't here. They told him as much as they knew. Then they ran away again down to the town. Somewhere he must be, somebody must have taken him in.

Peter sat down and thought, and then he left the house and turned up to the mountain. If he came and I wasn't here, he would go on, up to the top maybe where we used to sit and look down at the town and the sea. The snow was swirling. It was like fog. Fog on a mountain is a dreadful thing. There is no sense of direction. You can walk and walk and end up where you started. He called out, "Joe! Joe!" in a loud voice. The dog was beside him. "Find Joe," he said to the dog. The dog looked at him. "Go on, find Joe!" he said. The dog set off. If it was a sheep or a lamb, he thought, the dog might find him, but he has no scent for a human being. There could be no tracks. Even if there were tracks they would be blotted out as soon as they were made, by the wind and the flakes. He went up and up. Sometimes the wind blew away and he could see the top, so he had a sense of direction. But he had to walk warily, because the snow rested gently on deep bogholes that would swallow you, ones that you knew like the palm of your hand in ordinary times, even on black nights. If he came up here he is lost, he thought, and clenched his teeth.

It took him two hours to reach the top. He could only guess he was at the top from the strength of the wind coming from the sea. He stood there and called again, "Joe! Joe!" but the wind took his words and swept them away. The dog had left him. He didn't know where the dog was for the past hour. Then he heard him barking.

Joe was glad to feel the wet muzzle of the dog in his face even though he thought it was a dream and the dog was nuzzling him awake from a dream. He was burrowed into a cleft that was made by a dip and heather overhead. He hadn't much snow on him but he was very cold. He had gone there for shelter when the snow started to fall and then when he thought about the grey crows he had buried his face in his arms so that they wouldn't see his eyes if he was trapped like the sheep. He might even have started to go home when the snow fell but he was awful afraid of the grey crows and that they would pluck out his eyes. He was very pleased to feel the strong arms lifting him. "The door was closed," he told him, "and I thought mebbe you'd be up the hill looking at God." "Take it easy," Peter said. The face was flushed, the eyes were too bright. He stripped off his own short coat and waistcoat and he wrapped them around him. The snow felt cold on his shirt. "We're off home now, Joe," he said.

It took three hours to get down.

The dog didn't know his way. The swirling snow was too impenetrable. They must have walked the same way four times. You'd think all you had to do was to travel on the fall, but for all you knew you might be on the fall of the other side and be travelling towards the sea, because the wind shifted. You had to keep it in your back, but sometimes you would feel it in your face and didn't know whether it had shifted a bit or if you had changed your direction. Sometimes one leg went to the thigh in bog and he had to throw himself back with the boy high in his arms and pull his leg from the muck. He couldn't use his arms to free himself. There was no weight in Joe but after three hours there seemed to be the body of a grown man in his arms. He didn't really mind. All he wanted to do was to get Joe home.

He did.

They sent for the doctor. Peter waited until the doctor came and then he turned back to his own house. He was shivering. He didn't think Joe would survive it and he wanted to offer his own body, the strength of it, so that Joe could have some of it. But there's no way you can do that, is there?

Peter felt feverish the next morning. There was lassitude in his limbs. He put up a great fight, or did he? Anyhow it only took him four days to die. The doctor said he didn't want to live, you'd think. Joe's mother never closed an eye watching and tending in his house. But nothing could save him.

Joe grew. Even when he grew bigger, there was hardly a day that he didn't pass by the house at the butt of the mountain. The door was rotten and sagging. The thatched roof had fallen in. Joe never was robust, but Joe never forgot. Peter was always a song in his head, and he never failed to see him from the top of the hill.

The Wasteland

IT WAS A piece of ground that lay between the road that bounded the twin terrace of houses and the very high wall of the orchard. It wasn't a lovely piece of ground. Many of the inhabitants used it as a sort of convenient dumping place for unwanted articles of furniture or for pots and pans that had developed unmendable holes. Old rotting sacks also littered it, and piles of stones and rubble left over from the time long ago when they were building the houses. In the middle of the ground it was cleared of nearly everything in a roughly shaped quadrangle where the local children played football, and on the verges of this nettles and thistles grew strong and tall, intertwined with chickenweed and coarse grass and a few debilitated briars.

It was a good hot day and the quadrangle was occupied. The boys were playing football. It wasn't a real sort of leather football. It was a sheep's bladder that had been begged from the slaughterhouse, blown up, and tied at the neck. It made a good football. It was still fairly fresh so that it was heavy, and if you had to handle it, it was unpleasant to the touch; but you could close your nostrils so that the strong smell of it didn't altogether overpower you. There were twelve boys playing, six on each side. The two smallest boys were in goal. The goal-posts were tattered and bedraggled coats piled in bundles. The boys weren't well dressed. Most of them played in their bare feet. Some of them wore ragged trousers with the tails of their shirts peeping through holes in the seats of them. They screeched and shouted a lot. It was a common sight to see two boys nose to nose gesticulating with their hands and the veins on their necks inches thick as they shouted their protestations.

The rows didn't last long, because they were commanded by the biggest of the boys, who was the only one of them wearing long trousers. They were obviously the trousers belonging to a bigger brother which had been handed down, and although the waist was hitched chest-high and the bottoms dragged a little on the ground, they gave him an air of command and adulthood, so to speak, which, aided by his height and bulk, soon put an end to argument. They kept calling him Pongo and they referred every bit of strife to his mature judgement. It didn't take Pongo long to decide the case. If his decision favoured his own side, he came down weightily on that side, and put an end to the opposition by asking them if they wanted to fight. Since he had a mean sort of face and very big muscles, he always got his way.

At moments like this (the pugnacious ones) he always looked at the leader of the other section: a thin but lithe boy who had sandy-coloured hair standing up on his head, a narrow face with a humorous twitch at the lips and dark deep-set eyes. The boys called him Melia. There were certain times during the course of the game when Pongo thought that Melia was going to take up his challenge. This would have pleased Pongo very much, since he would be bound to win the fight and nothing pleased him more than to be thumping boys who were no match for him. As you see, Pongo wasn't at all a nice character.

Melia indeed many times considered resenting his decisions, but thought better of it. He was sensitive to pain. He had suffered pain before, of course, in the cause of justice, like the bloody nose that would be tender to the touch for days, or the black swollen eye, or the twisted arm that made it hard afterwards to fire stones with accuracy. All these things he knew he would have to suffer if he challenged bad decisions, and he couldn't take it, because he thought that pain never became a habit. It wasn't something that lessened with repetition. It was always fresh and excruciating, and suffering it often never, never softened its effects.

So what he couldn't get by force he was determined to get by guile. And there was no doubt about how well he could play with the ball. He was very fast on his feet and very tricky and he never was where you wanted him to be so that you could nail him, and Pongo was very annoyed that Melia could score goals by fleetness and cunning and actual honesty. So when the ball flew between his goals Pongo had to accept it, unless the ball went a fraction over the bundle of coats. Then he announced that it went one side of the posts and was therefore void. He himself scored goals by brute force, running and hopping the ball, and any little fellow who came within reach of his arm got a push that polished his trousers on the hard ground. But again Melia had a habit of coming from the side and the back and the front and robbing Pongo of the ball, until at times he was hard put to it to accept the robbery in a sportsmanlike way.

So now you will see what glee Pongo got out of the notebook.

It was when he himself had forced a goal against Melia's side, and in the scuffling the coats had been disturbed and kicked and Pongo threw himself down on them with his legs stretched out and said: "I'm tired now. We'll have a rest." They all obeyed his command and sat on the ground around him. Pongo's stretched hand found the notebook under his fingers, so he sat up and opened it. It was a small red notebook that you could buy for a penny, and he peered at it and turned it and scrutinised it until he could make out what was written on it. The biggest thing that was in it was Melia's name, which was nearly as highly decorated with curleycues and wriggles and designs as a lead letter in the Book of Kells. Then he turned the page and started to mutter the words with his lips until finally the light dawned on him and he sat up straight.

"Bejay!" he shouted then. "It's bloody poetry. Hey, fellas, it's Melia writing poetry."

That drew their attention. Melia had been stretched out not noticing. But he noticed now. He sat up. His face reddened in blotches as the skin of sandy-haired people usually does.

"Here, Pongo," he said, getting to his knees. "That's mine. Give it back."

"You'll get it back," Pongo said, "when we have it good and read."

"Give it back," said Melia rushing at him. But Pongo held him off with one arm while he got to his feet and then said: "All right, fellas, hold on to him."

They obeyed him cheerfully. They jumped on Melia from all sides. They were like octopi the way they wrapped themselves around his limbs.

"Listen to this," said Pongo, and Melia was frantic shouting at him: "Don't do it, Pongo. I'll kill you if you do it, Pongo. On me oath I'll kill you if you do it!"

"Gag him," said Pongo, and two or three dirty hands, smelling of dirt and refuse and stale sheep's bladder, were put over his mouth. It made him hold his breath.

Pongo wasn't an intellectual. Even though unfortunate teachers were trying to pound something into his head at school, Pongo would never be an intellectual. His highest flights of poetry were reached when he got through four lines of the parody on Casabianca:

> The boy stood on the burning deck
> His feet were full of blisters;
> The Captain sat in the public house
> With beer running down his whiskers.

So it was very strange now, and a cause of exquisite suffering to the boy Melia to hear these lines on Pongo's lips:

You see a boy with thin legs
In our field,
Touching the purple tips of thistles
With the palm of his hand.

In our field
You see a coloured bee scattering
The pollen of the burning nettle
Passing by.

In our field
You see small blue flowers
Pressing through the rusted hole
Of a pot:

And underneath a lifted bag
The hidden shoots of weeds are
White as snow
In our field.

That was as far as he got, because with a terrible strength
born out of mental suffering and agony, almost as when a heated
poker would be placed on an exposed nerve, Melia threw off
the boys that held him and he leaped on the big Pongo.

He was cursing as he leaped on him. His thin fists were
flying and his legs were kicking and his head was butting.
"You cockroach! You filthy moron! You unspeakable, lice-
ridden, son-of-a-bitch, I'll kill you! Oh if only God would put
a knife in my hand until I gutted you!"

He was doing well without the knife.

There was blood pouring from Pongo's nose and there was
blood on his lips and he was seeing stars, and since it was the
first time that this had ever happened to him he was afraid and
he shouted, "No! No!" and flat on his back he brought up his
arms to defend his face.

Melia had to stand back then of course and the fury left

him and he was very pale, but he had the notebook crushed in his hand.

"Don't ever do that again," he said. "Don't ever do that again."

And with the instinct of his kind Pongo knew that the fit had left Melia, so he sat up and then got to his feet and looked at him and he said, "You've done it now! I'm coming for you now!" and Melia, knowing that his fight was over and that there was no more water in his well, seeing the blood-flecked Pongo and his backers backing him up, just turned and ran with the pack on his heels.

He was a fleet runner. He dodged down the back lanes where the people left their dustbins. And he ran into the market place where the country people had their horses and carts and sacks of potatoes and cabbages and eggs that they were selling. He dodged a lot there, and finally when it was nearly evening he climbed the old shed where your man kept his rattletrap of a bus garaged. It had a flat roof and he lay there with his blue eyes (one of them sore and swollen) peering over the parapet. He saw and heard the searchers. They were well spread out. They shouted all the time: "Melia! We'll get you. Wherever you are, we'll get you. You won't go home until we get you." And Melia who was once again sensitive to pain, shivered. He could see the back of his house. They were waiting there for him. And he supposed they were waiting at the front. He could have run for it, but he didn't want to be beaten. He would wait patiently until his father came home from work and his few pints after work. His father would come home singing softly as he always did. A big man with a smile and wonderful stories vividly imagined. And Melia would call to him and he would be safe. His father would see him home. Melia felt his split lip and his closing eye and he thought of what had happened and he argued: Well, it was worth it, it was really worth it and I'd do the same again.

Only dimly did he understand that no wasteland can afford a poet.

Tuesday's Children

THE DOCTOR HEARD the clock striking midnight as he finished his last entry for Monday in the Diary. He felt very tired. He had had a long hard day. He looked at the virgin whiteness of Tuesday and he prayed that it would remain that way. He heard his wife calling him from upstairs. "All right, all right, I'm coming now," he shouted. Then he rose, stretched himself, switched off the light and walked slowly up the stairs. He thought of the time he was a student when he played football and stayed up half the night at dances, and even after drinking quite a bit, the way he could awake in the morning without a bad head. He thought back to those days with wonder. He tried to see himself running a hundred yards with a ball. He couldn't imagine it any more. He was too tired. He wondered what devil had inspired him to take up the art of healing.

He was at the top of the stairs, his fingers on the light switch, when the front-door bell rang. "Oh, no!" he groaned. He wondered if he would pretend not to hear. If he stayed quiet would the caller go away? It was a point he had debated often with himself. He was always the loser. He knew he would have to go down and open the door, but every tired nerve of him was rebelling against it. He cursed with all the fluidity of his student days, more biting now with maturity, and then he went down and took the latch off the front door, opened it, shoved his greying head out and barked, "Well, what is it?"

The man outside was unperturbed.

"Good night, Doctor," he said. "Would you come? Herself is having it hard."

The doctor looked at him. A small stocky man with a big chest and a black unshaven face, with white teeth and a few of them missing. An unprepossessing character with an ingratiating smile.

"What's wrong with her?" the doctor asked.

"Dunno," said the man. "Just she's having it hard. Never hard with any of the others."

"How many others?" the doctor asked.

"Nine," the man grinned, almost pouting his chest. "Six died."

"All right," the doctor said. "I'll be with you." He went back in for his bag, thinking over what he would need. Six died, eh? he was thinking. No wonder. You could deliver them safely, but what happened afterwards in those tents and camps, with dogs and cats and horses and ponies and malnutrition? It's a wonder more of them didn't die.

He went out.

He got into his car, opened the other door.

"Get in," he said to the tinker. The man got in. The doctor could smell the heat of him. It wasn't a hot night. The man was sweating. He saw that his hand had a tremble in it. It was an enormous dirty hand, very muscular. A tremble was alien to it.

"Who delivered all the others?" he asked as he swung the car out of the avenue.

"Herself and meself," the man said.

"You're an expert so," the doctor said. "Why do you want me?"

"This is different," the man said. "This is different. This is hard. Been together a long time we have, meself and herself. She's all right. It would be bad to lose her. You understand."

The doctor was moved.

156

"She should probably go to hospital," he said. Too late now, he thought. He lived way out in the country. The hospital was miles away.

"Oh, no," the man said. "No hospital. Killers, them hospitals."

"I'm too tired to give you a lecture on hygiene and modern medicine," the doctor said.

The car swung out of the doctor's road and right into a bad road which led away into bleak places. He saw the tent at the side of the road in the headlights of the car. It was a round tent built under the shelter of the horse cart. He brought the car close to it and left the headlights burning.

"She's in here," the man said, going on his knees and lifting the flap.

The doctor got on his knees too and crawled in with his bag. It was too small for the three of them. He saw the woman's agony in the light of a candle. Her face was soaked with sweat and her black hair limp from it. She raised her head and looked.

"I got him, Leel," the man said. "Everything is fine now, you see."

"Hello," she said. She had a very strong face, he saw, big jawbones, high cheekbones, well burned from the sun but pale under the tan.

This is terrible, the doctor was thinking. The small tent was fugged. He felt sweat breaking out all over his body. He had to struggle out of his coat. There was a smell that could be almost cut with a knife of humans and dogs too who had lain on the place in the daytime.

Three hours later, he still thought it was impossible. The woman should have died. Her baby should have died. Nobody should have to work under conditions like that. The battery of his car was practically burned out, but he felt good. He had done something that was, or should have been, impossible.

"No more," he said to the man as he sat in his car. "Next time she dies. You understand that."

The man's face fell.

"I mean it," the doctor said. "You've had it, that's that."

"I'll look after her," the man said. "What do I owe you, Doctor?"

The doctor thought. He laughed. "Say a prayer for me," he said.

"God bless you," the man replied. "Is that all right?"

"That'll do fine," said the doctor.

"Here," said the man then, reaching into a pocket and handing him a small carved piece of ebony. "Take that. It's good luck. Long as you have that in the house, none of your children will ever get the croup. It's good. Old granny had that. Came down from way back, from Europe, from the world. All right?"

"All right," said the doctor. He drove away. He was very amused. He chuckled all the way home.

When he got in, the telephone was ringing.

He was conditioned now. He raised the receiver without even an inward curse. He was turning the piece of ebony in his hand. It was roughly carved but had been worn smooth by generations of fingers. An ugly sort of faceless god, seated, with hands held up.

It was a call from a nursing home in the town, all of twenty miles away. He was to come quickly. Mrs B. had just gone in. Were they sure it was time for him? Was she really on the verge? She was. He was very tired. He saw no stimulation from Mrs B. She was wealthy. She was as healthy as a river trout. "All right," he said tiredly, "I'll come."

When if ever would he catch up on his sleep? he wondered, as he drove to the town. Once or twice he found himself nodding and had to pull himself awake and swerve the car from the verge of the road.

Mrs B. wasn't ready, but she wanted him. She was white and pink, a picture in the spotless bed under the bright lights. There were flowers in the room. It was very elegant. She reached her hand for him. "Thank God you have come," she said, "I couldn't have lived if you hadn't come." He smiled at her, thinking hard things, how she wouldn't be ready for hours yet and he could have been at home in bed sleeping. "Everything will be all right," he said automatically.

There was nothing to it.

He snatched half-hour naps down on the hard couch in the waiting room. His mind was whirling with black faces and white teeth, and the stoical woman in the tent, her jaw muscles tightening under the pain of the things he had to do to her, without any anaesthetic worth while. She had a brave face, that Leel.

Mrs B. was shouting for "something." You'll have to give me something. I can't bear it. I can't bear it. "Later, later," he'd say. Then she wouldn't let him slip away for a nap. He smoked too many cigarettes. His mouth felt like a rush mat. Dawn had come and the after dawn and midday before he was ready to leave for home. Later than that. There was nothing to it. The contortions and agonies of Mrs B., and she a fine strong woman who shouldn't have suffered more than ordinary.

Her husband in the waiting room. Very well dressed, with an expensive stomach on him, a red and purple nose. Drinking too much, the doctor thought to himself. If he doesn't stop he'll die soon from the effects of a fatty heart. How is she? And don't leave her. She wants you every minute. Great God, you'd think the most famous person in the world was being born instead of a soft fat pink and white little girl who would be a sister to the son and grow up with too much money all around her and be completely spoiled. He couldn't help thinking of the thin whippetlike baby that he had helped into the world earlier. Holding on to life with thin thumbs. Does life have to be so cynically contrasting so that it forces itself on your attention?

It was late afternoon by the time that he was ready to leave. All but half an hour of it wasted time, and time and life so short. Mrs B.'s room was a mound of flowers and fruit and gifts with one or two perfumed relatives walking around hushed. You'll come back tomorrow. Yes, yes, in the morning. Goodbye now. Everything will be all right. Everything will be all right. It was like the refrain of a popular song sung so often that you were sick and tired of it. But after all it was a living. If it wasn't for Mrs B. you couldn't help a person like Leel and all you demanded was a prayer. It was just a different set of circumstances, that was all.

He was about to turn from the village street into his own road when he shoved on the brakes and pulled the car to a screaming stop. He got out of it. He was very angry. He walked over to her. There was Leel with a multicoloured shawl around her and the baby enveloped in it. She was going into a shop.

"Here," he shouted, "what's the idea? What's the bloody idea? Do I haul you back from the grave to have you digging a new one? You shouldn't be here. You should be at home in bed."

As soon as he said it, he thought of what he had said. At home. In bed. In bed with Mrs B. He tried to place Leel in Mrs B.'s room.

"Sure it's nothing, Doctor," said Leel, anxiously. "I haven't time to be staying in bed. I've never stayed in bed before. What would I be doing in bed?"

His anger faded away. What was the use? God gave bodies to people to abuse or use. She looked terrible but she was on her feet. Nothing he could say was any good.

"All right," he said wearily. "I told you. At least I told you." He went back to the car. My God, it was incredible.

"God bless you," she called after him. "The blessings of God on you."

It sounded mechanical. It was the formula used by grateful beggars who might be laughing at you behind their hands. It didn't mean anything. Nothing meant anything. The longer you lived and the more you saw, the less you understood.

When he got home his wife was waiting for him. She was anxious about him. She had his meal nicely laid out and a cheerful fire burning. He thanked God for her. "You must be tired," she said. "I'm sorry it was so hard, the day."

"That's right," he said.

The telephone rang.

"Who is it?"

"It's Mr B."

"Mr B. Well, what do you want? She has a headache, has she. Well, she's damn lucky if that's all she has. Let her put up with it. I have a headache and what can I do about it? No, I can't come back in, I don't care how much she wants me. How much can the body of a human being stand? I just saw a woman this minute who had a baby this morning. Do you know what she was doing? She was out walking. If your wife went through a tenth of what she went through she would be dead now. That's true. No. I won't go in now. I'll see your wife in the morning or not at all. She's as healthy as a trout. There's nothing wrong with her. I know there isn't. That's all. Goodbye. Goodbye."

He banged it down.

"That's that," he said. "Another client gone."

He pulled out his diary.

He broke its virginity with a scratching pen.

"To a tinker," he wrote, "a son. To a rich man, a daughter." And under that he wrote viciously in capitals: THESE WERE TUESDAY'S CHILDREN.

Hallmarked

◆◇◆

MICHAEL JOHN SOLD everything.

He could see you in and see you out of the world, simple or de luxe, at both ends at a fair price and no middlemen. While you were in it he could sustain you with food or drink for man, child or beast, of any sex, creed or generation. He could post a letter for you that would go several times around the world if you wanted, or by speaking at the bit of wire he could let you talk to His Holiness the Pope in Rome if the man wasn't too busy to have a chat with you.

It was the only shop in the village and it sold everything. Strangers rarely found their way into it. It was in the middle of the mountains down a glen that bore a river that was running mad for the sea. It was a long bad road that led into it from the main road, too rocky and potholed for posh cars, too hilly for bicycles, too uninviting for shank's mare. Everyone in it was quite happy as far as happiness goes, and they didn't care if they never saw a stranger. But if one came they could put up with him and tell him what was happening where he came from because they were great people for knowing everything, having wireless sets and weekly papers and legions of relations in America who sent them big bundles of glossy magazines and hair-raising comics that they read themselves but kept away from the childer because most of the lassies in the pictures were more than half naked and were showing more of their bumps to the world than a rawhide cow, bless the mark.

So Michael John was a little surprised one fine spring

morning looking out his small windowpane while he was rubbing a pint glass, to see a stranger coming out of the crutch of the hill and walking down the main road. He was a tall man dressed in a dark suit. The boots he was wearing and the bottoms of his trousers were covered in dust. He's come far, Michael John thought wisely, and he walked it. There was a great breadth of shoulder on him and he had very long arms hanging straight down. They were almost below his knees. His head was bare and his short hair was very grey and there was a sort of yellow look about his face. He paused in the middle of the road. There were only four houses to be seen. The other few were hidden over the shoulder of the hills. He saw the nearly obliterated sign about licence to sell tobacco outside Michael John's and he headed that way. Michael John pulled away from the window. The shop was part of the house. He had a small piece of a counter and the big open fire was blazing, because even though it was a spring day there was snow on the top of the hills and you would be frozen if you weren't working. A few barrels and a few chairs and all the rest shelves holding his goods. You'd wonder how in the name of God he knew where to lay his hands on things, but he did.

The man darkened the door.

"Good day," said Michael John.

The man came in. He could see his face. All expression seemed to be wiped out of it. A big face, with bulging muscles on the jaws and a strong nose. Calm brown eyes, that seemed to have no expression in them either. Michael John liked the man from the look of him. That was the way he was. He would like you or not. If he liked you and you turned out bad he would always find excuses for you. If he didn't like you and you turned out to be a saint he would question the choir of angels that worked the miracles in your name.

"It's a nice day," said the man. His voice seemed to be rusty.

"It is, thank God," said Michael John.

"Thank God again," said the man.

"I'd like to buy a loaf of bread and a little cheese and a bottle of stout," he said.

"It's a pleasure," said Michael John reaching for them.

"Would it offend you if I eat them here?" the man asked.

"It would not," said Michael John. He thought the man had good manners anyhow.

He watched the man eating. He ate slowly and carefully. He chewed every bit of the bread and cheese slowly and washed it down his throat with the stout. He took a purse out of his pocket then and he extracted a few coins and he paid, and Michael John thought he was old-fashioned. Very few men carried the little leather purses nowadays. He wasn't as young as he had looked walking to the house. Michael John thought he would be more than fifty. But well set up still. Muscles were bulging his coat sleeves. He had no spare flesh on him. Michael John was puzzled by him.

He cut tobacco and filled a pipe and lighted it. Then he looked at Michael John.

"This is a nice spot," he said. "Is it lonely?"

"I don't know," said Michael John. "We like it. Is it lonely? I don't know. We haven't time to be lonely."

"I don't mean that way," said the man. "I mean many strangers don't find their way into it."

"We're rarely troubled," said Michael John.

"When I came in by the fork on the hills," said the man, "I saw a green space up in the middle of the heather. There is a house there too with a latch on it. Like it was a small farm carved out of the hills that was left to lie."

"That's right," said Michael John. "That's a place."

"Does it belong to people?" he asked.

"It belongs to me," said Michael John. "I was born in that house. Me grandfather died in it. We couldn't shift him down here."

That paused the man. His big hands rubbed against each other.

"Would you let me live there?" he asked. Out. Direct.

Michael John was nonplussed.

"It's not in good shape," he said. "The thatch is bad. It must be leaking inside. There'd want to be an awful lot done to it."

"I'll do it," said the man. "I'll do all that wants to be done to it, and I'll clear the fields of the ferns and the gorse that's grown up in it. I'll make it very tidy for you and I'll pay you within my means."

"It's a long way from company," said Michael John. "In the bad winter there's no way out of it. A person'd be snowed up like the sheep."

"I'd like it that way," said the man.

"Where are you from?" Michael John asked.

"I'd like not to tell you that," the man said earnestly. "I'd just like to fix that little house and let me go in there and no sinner know about me. I could tell you I'm from here or there but I don't want to tell you. Just that if you think I'm honest you will oblige me, and if you don't think so just let it lie."

Michael John thought. He looked into the brown eyes that were calmly fixed on his own. Michael John had a big, cheerful, ugly face that was very readable. The man knew he had succeeded when he saw the crinkling eyes.

"All right," said Michael John.

A soft sigh escaped from the man. Michael John was surprised. A terrible lot depended on that, he thought.

"My name is Paul," said the man.

"Shake on it so, Paul," said Michael John holding out his hand.

Paul seemed to hesitate, and then put out his hand. It was as hard as rock, Michael John felt.

"You do it up, and when you have it fixed we can talk about a payment from then," said Michael John. "Up to that it will be like you are working for me."

The man looked his thanks. For one of the few times in his life Michael John was embarrassed at the gratitude looking out of the man's eyes. That look should only be in the eyes of a sick dog, he thought.

If the people wanted something to talk about they had it now. They wanted to know everything. Michael John knowing very little more than themselves had to pretend to be very mysterious. That went well. Just a friend of mine, said Michael John, from the other side of the country. Bad health. Building himself up.

In three months you wouldn't know the small place on the side of the hill. From being sad and decayed and green-moulded the house became yellow and white and glittering. The man never seemed to stop working. Under a spade the hard little fields groaned off their green and the cleared rocks became neat stone walls all around them. It was like a miracle on the side of a hill. The fairies couldn't have done better. But nobody could get close to the fellow. He would return your greeting and agree about the weather and drink a bottle with you in Michael John's in the calm of the evening. But that's all. His name was Paul. He had lost his yellow look. He was brown and strong and one of the hardest-working men they had ever met. And one of the happiest. The contentment that flowed out of the man was even enough to kill your curiosity. They became fond of him, and proud of his place, and Michael John became possessive about him, as if he had got him from Santa Claus for Christmas.

The inside of the house was good. The furniture he made himself wasn't crude. It was smooth and well made and solid like himself. The kids liked him. Apparently they understood his silence. He could make the queerest yokes with a knife that you ever saw out of bits of bogdeal or the roots of briars. There wasn't a kid in the place that didn't have one of them.

The parents often questioned the children about him. What did he say? (Arrah, nothin'.) What did he do? (Arrah, nothin'.) Eventually they gave up probing and just accepted him.

Until the motor car made its way into the mountains the following spring.

If you stood on the top of the hills and looked down at it you would be appalled at the terrible struggle it was having. It jolted and bumped and swayed, and steam came from under it like a monster. It wasn't the only car that had come in there. Lorries had come before and often did to bring supplies in to Michael John. But lorry drivers are very reckless people and would drive a lorry in and out of hell as long as they didn't own it themselves.

Paul was working at the roadway he was making into the place. It was a cruel hard job, but he had conquered the boggy bits and the granite bits and it was a pleasant path to look at running up and hugging the contours of the hillside. He saw the car making its way and he leaned on the spade to watch it come. If he had seen it a year ago coming it might have given him uneasiness, but he was a different man now. There was nothing before him but his life. He had buried the years that were gone in his sweat.

The man driving the car was small and tubby. He could no longer see his crotch for his stomach. He had rimless glasses and his face was a round blob that was decorated with a small nose and a small mouth and small eyes. He travelled for people. He sold all sorts of things for them. He was very successful because he often did what he was doing now, following the bad byroads that other men would have thought too much trouble.

As the steaming, groaning car came closer, Paul pretended to be working away. But he couldn't kill the curiosity and looked back now and again over his shoulder. The car stopped below him with a lurch. The window rolled down. He heard the small high voice calling him. He turned and ambled down to stand beside the car. He could feel the heat from it. Then he saw the face of the little man and his life was destroyed. The man tried to cover the recognition in his face, but it was too late. Paul had seen it. Bitterness flooded over him and a black despair. His hands tightened on the spade. The man was frightened when he saw the white beside his nostrils. Then Paul turned away and went trudging up the hill. The little fat fellow called after him, to cover up.

"Hi, mister, is this the way in to Michael John's?"

The man didn't turn back to answer him. He kept striding up the hill.

He let in the clutch and went on.

He was gleeful. Who'd ever believe? He heard himself telling the story in the commercial room of every tuppenny hapenny hotel in the country. The twist and the build-up and the climax. Did these people in here know? What do you bet they didn't know? I bet you a fiver they don't know. Wait'll they hear. Man, who'd have thought in the middle of a wilderness like this? He went down into the valley at speed. He didn't notice the tumbling river, the glittering sea in the distance, the sun shining brightly on the white-faced cottages, the heather of the hills throwing off the frost, the sedge shooting green shoots. He saw nothing because he was really only a little blind man who thought about nothing except commission and dirty stories.

Michael John was in the shop, and two more of the men.

He didn't try to sell anything even. He started straight off.

"Hey! How are ye, men. I met a fella up on the side of the hill. Know who he was?"

"That's Paul," said Michael John.

"Paul, my aunt Fanny!" said the little fat fellow. "That's James Brian that killed his wife twelve years ago, down in the town. Came home drunk he did and didn't know his own strength. Listen, man. Listen to the cream of it. Know who was foreman of the jury that convicted him? Me! Imagine that? Did you ever hear the like of that?"

"Listen," said Michael John tensely, "did you talk to him?"

"No fear," said the little fellow. "Not me. Talk to a murderer, is it? He took one look at me and he went up the hill as if the devil was after him."

Michael John left the shop at a run. He was cursing and cursing. He wasn't built for running any more. He was slow in the legs and heavy around the waist but he ran. Up the road and around towards the curve of the hill, holding his hand at his chest to stop his heart from bursting. His tongue was hanging out on his cheek like a pointer dog in the heather.

And he was too late. That was what he was afraid of.

He stood there and called to the small figure down in the valley. The small figure of the big man leaping down. He had the suit on that he came with and nothing at all in his hands or in his pockets or on his back. He was going out the very same way he came in. Michael John stood there and called: "Paul! Paul!" He called and the hills carried his call away and over the man and threw it off the hills and sent it back to him. He saw the figure of the man stand as if he had been hit with a bullet, hesitate and then run on. Michael John shouted "Paul!" once more, but it was no use, and he knew it was no use. Tears of anger and sadness came into his eyes and he had to bend in two coughing from the way the breath was strangling in him from the unaccustomed running. And then when the spasm was finished he turned and walked back to the group at the door of the shop.

The little fat one saw him looking at him with red-rimmed eyes.

"Get out of here, you little bastard," said Michael John. "And if you put a foot in this place again I'll shoot you."

"Now look here," said the little fellow with the bounce he

used to sell people things they didn't want.

"Get out of here," Michael John roared at him, scrabbling at his shoulder and pushing him towards his car. "Get out of here while you have unlet blood in you, you ball of filth, before I cripple you."

"But –" said the fellow, and then after a look at Michael John's face he leaped into the car and shot away. Michael John bent and took up a rock from the road and flung it at the car. It bounced off the black paint leaving a dint in it.

Then the anger left his face. His clenched hands unloosed themselves.

He walked into the shop. He went over towards the fire, He sat on a stool there and he lowered his face into his hands.

The Eyes of the Cat

◄◊►

THE FIGHT DIDN'T last very long.

The girl walking down the steps of the hotel in the Square was attracted first by the sight of the running men.

It was drawing towards evening. There was nothing left of the great fair, except the ragtag and bobtail. The Corporation cleaners were already out hosing away the dung and litter of the day. The hoses were not perfect. Their long lengths leaked and threw up delicate fountains of water so that many passersby cursed them and the cleaners and the Corporation.

It was back behind the girl's car that the crowd was converging, excitement in their eyes, making a ring. Old calves, unsold, were left bleating as their owners deserted them. Old and weary cows hung their heads and longed for the green pastures.

She stepped into the open red sports car and stood on the seat. She could see over the heads of the people. Her pulse was unaccountably hammering. There were three men in the cleared space. One of them stood tall and straight and disdainful, moving delicately like a cat as the other two circled him swinging heavy blackthorn sticks in their hands. He had no weapon.

The two men were big. One of them had thrown his coat on the dirty street. His upper body was bare and burned by the sun and his chest and arms were matted with black hair. His arms bulged with his grip on the stick. The other aggressor was bareheaded and younger. Ginger hair stood up on his head. He was drunk and staggering, and the obscenities that poured out of him were gobbled so that their point was lost. I would be afraid of the big black one, she thought. He had almost a week's old bristle and wore a red scarf around his bare throat. He wasn't very drunk and he wasn't cursing.

The man whom they stalked was bigger than either of them. His blond hair was thick and the front of it bleached almost white. His skin was honey-coloured from the touch of the sun, like all fair people. He wore a white shirt that lacked all its buttons so that it opened down to the brass buckle of his belt. The sleeves of the shirt were chopped off high and the cloth was stretched tightly over the muscles of his arms. He held his arms up, his fists clenched, the broad strap on his right wrist making the veins stand out on his arm.

She almost screamed a warning as the black one moved. He moved very fast. One moment he was circling and the next he had dodged and leaped and the stick swung high and fell. The blond man was not quite quick enough. He had to keep his eyes on both of them at the same time. His left arm raised to take most of the blow, but the knob of the stick glanced off his forehead and almost immediately a scarlet stream of blood started to pour down the side of his face and dripped onto his bare chest. The girl held her breath. The bantering crowd was silenced.

Then the redhead moved. He tried to emulate his partner, but something went wrong, because the blond man moved first, leaped beyond him, caught a fistful of his coat, swung him around, hit him a dull crunching blow in the face, bent down, caught him by the fork with his striking hand, raised him high and flung him bodily at the black one who was coming in. The crowd scattered.

The black man cursed, lying on the ground with the unconscious redhead binding him there. He pushed him off and got to his knees. He was too late. The tall blond fellow bent, took his blackthorn stick from the ground, raised it and hit him on the back of the head. It wasn't a savage blow. It was a calculated blow. The black man, groaned and brought up his hands to his head and pulled up his legs and lay there in the dust.

The blond fellow raised the stick in his two hands, bent it like a bow, strained. Something had to give. The heavy seasoned stick broke in two. He flung the pieces on the groaning body of his enemy, turned, made his way through the lane that opened for him and walked towards the girl in the car.

He didn't see her until he was close to her.

She saw him.

He seemed to cover a lot of ground with his long stride. She should have sat down and driven away. She didn't know what stopped her. His breathing seemed to be unhurried. She could see the cut in his forehead still oozing a little blood. It flowed down avoiding his eye, down by the side of the big jaw that was bulging with muscle. She thought she had never seen a braver face. His eyes were very blue, very clear, very calm. The nose was straight and inclined towards rather thick lips over a square chin. He was very big. She thought she had never seen anyone like him. Her eyes were glued on him.

When he came to the back of the car his eyes met hers. They held her own eyes and then slowly travelled down her. She felt she was standing up on the seat for his inspection. The eyes of the man saw a girl with black, black hair, so black that it was almost blue, straight black eyebrows under a broad forehead. High cheekbones with the eyes sunken back, narrowed under his scrutiny. She was well built. An expensive grey costume was well cut to show her body. A fine body. The car keys were swinging in her hand. He came over close and placed his hand on the door of the car.

She could smell him then. The smell of sweat from him and fresh blood and the smell of horses. The stripe of scarlet blood on his chest looked like a decoration.

It's a coarse face, she thought then. It is a coarse, rather brutal face after all. She was afraid. Because she wanted to step out of the car and go close to him and feel the heavy arms around her. Her thumping heart was driving up black dots in front of her eyes. She couldn't pull her eyes away from his.

A voice behind calling.

"Beat it, Gib! Beat it, Gib! The police are on the way," the voice was calling.

He took his hand off the car door and went on. She sank down in the seat. Her mouth was dry. She felt drained of all emotion. The hand on the car door she thought then had been well shaped, but the fingers were very broad and the nails cracked and broken and dirty, but she could see still the small fair hair on the back of the hand, and she wondered what it would be like to feel the back of the hand rubbing against the side of her cheek.

Am I mad? Am I mad? she wondered then. What has come over me? She looked and saw him walking towards the light tinker's cart near the bottom of the Square. There was a shawled woman up there holding the reins. He leaped onto the cart, took the reins, bent forward and hit the horse heavily on the flank with the flat of his hand. The horse leaped away. The car joggled crazily on its high springs before it settled down. Then it turned the corner and was gone from sight just as the two blue uniformed men came hurrying into the Square.

Thank God, he's gone, said her mind. Thank God, he's gone. She saw with wonderment that her fingers were trembling, that she had difficulty fitting the key into the ignition.

"What was wrong with them gangsters?" Gib's mother asked when they were clear of the town after racing the horse and cart through many side roads to dodge pursuit.

"Them," he said. "I sold them a horse."

She laughed.

"The Pinto, was it?" she asked.

"Yes," he said. "Some of the paint came off. I thought we'd ha' been clear before the paint kem off."

"It's half the price of them," she said. "Their own cousin sold us a lurcher last spring at Ballinasloe. It's half the price of them. I hope it keeps fine for them."

Later the red sports car passed them travelling fast.

It nearly didn't pass.

She recognised them with horror when she was close to them. She was wearing sun glasses. That's why it took so long to recognise them.

The car passed them by, and she didn't know it but as it passed them it slowed down as if something was pulling at its tail; then with a great effort it seemed to pull away again little by little until it went around the next corner in a cloud of dust. The girl's head was bent low to the wheel and she was breathing fast.

"You saw that one?" he asked.

"I did," said the old woman.

"I saw her in the Square," he said. "She was looking at the fight. I came over to her. I felt strings out of her."

"So well," said the old woman. "So well."

"What," he said. "You know her?"

"You know what they say," she went on. "You know what they say in the old language: Its origin breaks through the eyes of the cat. She has black eyes that one. And black hair."

"So," he said musing.

"We pass their place another few miles," she said. "A big place. Two hundred acres. Great cattle. Fat land. Very rich, the Man is. You know the Man?"

"I heard of him," he said. "Great God, yes, I heard of him. He was of us. Time ago he was of us."

"He was, faith. He was of us. Now he's off us." She laughed. "He calls the police now, if a gypsy puts a foot over his fence.

Own cousin of me own well back. But well back. Great black man he was. Great black man. He riz out of it. Time the last war in the world, he starts selling a few beasts. Then more and more beasts. Big man he became. The curved tent on the side of the road wasn't big enough to hold him."

"And that's why, that's why," said Gib. He opened his mouth and laughed. "She looked frightened," he said then through sharply pointed teeth. "Frightened she looked and then her eyes open and you see the green fields in them. She is his daughter so?"

"She is his daughter," said the woman. "It's the blood. The blood."

"Up the road it is, the place?"

"Yes. We come to it. Big tall gates, man. Very powerful the the Man is. Very powerful. Makes you laugh to see him in a striped suit and a white collar and big black car. Oh, dear, dear."

They came to the big iron gates. He stopped the cart.

He could see the neat gravelled drive curving away through the park. Up beyond he could see the big two-storey house. Red and white cattle grazing. A well kept place.

He threw her the reins. He jumped onto the road.

"Its origin breaks through the eyes of the cat," he said.

"That's right," said the old woman.

He tightened his belt. He bared his teeth.

"I'll maybe pay a call," he said.

"Don't let the Man see you," she said. "The Man is very powerful."

"I don't want to see the Man," he said. "I want to look into the eyes of the cat."

Then he was gone. He went in the gates and dropped low and squirmed his big body fast and sure into a belt of trees.

The old woman laughed. She took an old clay pipe from the recesses of her many garments, applied a match to it. The horse bent and cropped at the green grass at the side of the road. The old woman spat. Then she laughed.

"The eyes of the cat, indeed," she said.

Foreign Fish

—————◇—————

BARTLEY WAS GOING to bed when the knock came on the front door.

He was at the yawning stage, stretching himself, rubbing the back of his head with his big hands and scratching himself under the arms. The knock left him with his big body naked and his mouth half open.

"Who the hell is that?" Bartley asked the room. The men in this Irish seacoast town made their living fishing, and at this hour they were all sure to be in their beds, or well on their way, as Bartley was.

His wife was in the kitchen, raking the fire before coming in to bed. She appeared now.

He started to pull on his trousers. "See who's at the door," he told her.

"Me, is it," she said.

"What?" said Bartley. "Are you afraid? Do you expect the fairies or the ghost of your grandfather?"

"It's very late," she said. She was a nervous woman anyhow. Nice but nervous. Bartley laughed.

"You're still full of pishrogues," he told her, "for all your years. Well, I'll go down and see who it is."

"Who could it be at this hour of the night?" she asked him as he went down.

"I'll tell you when I find out," said Bartley, opening the door. He filled the whole opening, he was so big. She couldn't see out any side of him. But she heard him say, "Well, for God's sake, Melia, what do you mean rattling us up at this

181

hour of the night? Is it frightening the life out of us you are?"

He stepped aside, and Melia came past him. He was a middling-sized man, almost invisible in the blackness of the night, with his blue jersey and his fisherman's cap and his coat collar turned up. There was a bundle of white in his arms. They stared at it when it moved. It was a small, white, terrier pup nuzzling into his chest. Melia's thin face was bright as he looked at the little dog.

"Isn't he smashin'?" Melia asked. "Isn't he a little beauty?"

"Now listen, Melia," said Bartley, closing the door so that they were shut in with the friendly yellow light of the paraffin lamp. "If you got us all up in the middle of the night to admire another stray pup, I won't be responsible for me actions."

"Isn't he nice, ma'am?" asked Melia of Bartley's wife.

Her face softened, of course, and she came over to pat the pup's head. He was an extremely dirty little pup and looked half-starved.

"Wuff-wuff," said Mrs Bartley, scratching his head. "I'll get him a supeen of milk," she said then.

"Great God!" ejaculated Bartley.

"Out the road I found him," said Melia. "He was down on the beach near the sea. Cryin' away, he was. It took me a long time to find him among the white rocks."

"Melia," said Bartley, "I'm waitin' for you."

"Ah, leave the poor man alone," said the woman.

"There's a poacher out beyond, Bartley," said Melia.

"Are you sure, man?"

"I'm certain," said Melia. "He's trawling off the shore, and the wind is right. You remember what you said. Well, he's in the right spot now with the right wind for us to get up on him."

"God be praised," said Bartley rushing back into the bedroom.

Mrs Bartley was nervous. She handed the saucer of milk to Melia. She went to the bedroom door.

"Now, Bartley," she said, "don't rush away. He will be gone when ye get out to him. Leave it alone, Bartley, I tell you. Aren't they always in the bay? When the government won't do anything about them, why should ye? Aren't they part of life, like midges in the summer?"

"Is your boat ready, Melia?" Bartley shouted down.

"It is," said Melia back to him. "We were going out on the morning tide."

"Can you rattle up the sons now?" Bartley asked.

"They won't be best pleased," said Melia, "since they're so newly married and fond of the beds – but I'll get them out."

"You're a rattler man," Bartley shouted at him. "Go so, and get them and stir up Finbar Daly, and I'll get Shunter out with his boat."

"I will now," said Melia, "when your man here has his milk. Aren't you a good chap?" he asked the pup, who wagged a small tail.

Bartley came down, pulling on a jersey. He reached for the sea boots behind the door and sat down to pull them on. His thick, grey hair was disturbed on his head. His face was deeply coloured from the weather. His wife in her worry thought what a fine man he looked still and thought of his belly as flat as a board.

"You won't listen to me, I suppose," she said then.

"I will, of course," said Bartley. "But this is important. We've had this planned for a long time. Just waiting for the wind and the boat at the right time. Nothing much will happen. We'll creep up on them and we'll board them and we'll bate them a bit with our fists and then we'll bring in the boat and that's all there's to it. Other poachin' bogars might take warning from that."

"That's the man," said Melia to the dog, who was trying to

lick the glaze off the saucer. "Come on, now." He bent and lifted up the pup.

"You're sure about this now, Melia?" Bartley asked. "All the others will be rippin' if we're wrong."

"I'm sure," said Melia, and they knew it was right because that's the kind of man he was. "I'll go and collect the others now. It's a cold welcome I'll be gettin'." He chuckled. "But I'll rouse them out. See you below the quay, Bartley."

Bartley wasn't long after him. He went into the cold, blowy night leaving the warm, inviting house and the anxious eyes of his wife behind him.

The tide in the estuary was on the ebb, but there was still enough of it to raise the stumpy masts of the pucaun boats over the quay. Bartley roused his own son, John, on the way. He banged with his big fist on the windowpane of the bedroom and roared at him. That's how he got him up. He left when he heard him grumbling. He was more polite at Shunter's house. He kicked at the front door with his rubber boot and called softly, as he thought. You could have heard him over in the Islands. Shunter told him this forcibly, also many other blasphemous things so that his wife hid her ears under the patchwork quilt. Bartley laughed and went on his way.

Soon there was activity on the quaysides. Bartley was the only cheery man of them. Melia didn't mind, but the others grumbled a lot. They shivered in the raw air of the night. The wind wasn't strong but it was very harsh, like frozen fingers touching your skin. It was a shock after a warm bed that you had barely time to embrace. They told Bartley this. They told him he was a madman. He banged their backs for them and roared and laughed and made them even madder with his jollity. Bartley didn't mind. He told them they could take it out on the foreign poachers when they caught them.

There was a cold moon coming up behind them from the

Dublin direction as the four sturdy black boats swung away into the estuary. They had no trouble getting away. They brought nothing with them but their feelings and their fists — twelve men of them, mostly big, with hard hands and weatherbeaten faces, and the smoldering resentment that the foreign poachers aroused in all of them because they felt so helpless.

The boats slid along very silently, except for a creak of a block on the big brown sail or the lap of the side wind before they turned up north into the bay and had the wind chasing their tails.

They hugged the land. The land was black. The sea had a very faint colour, a light black-green color, laced by the single band of light on the horizon. They followed the leader.

Bartley and Melia and Finbar Daly and Shunter were at the tillers. Their sons or helpers manned the sail or peered ahead into the night or sat on the neatly laid, limestone ballast, blocks to get away from the cut of the wind. They said what they would do to Melia if this was a false alarm. Shunter said it wasn't really Melia that was to blame but big Bartley, and that he was the man to hang if this night was fruitless.

They knew what to do. They had spent many hours and drunk many barrels of porter over the years, working out what they would do if the opportunity arose. Bartley and Melia, with the wind behind them, would drive straight for the side of the trawler nearest the wind. The young men would grab the sides with an anchor or a gaff and hold on while the four men boarded. The other two boats would go around the other side, drop their sails and close with the boat if she turned to make off to the north. Between them they would get aboard her, eight fighting fishermen, with the resentment of the long years burning in them. They would bring in the poacher if they had to die in the attempt.

They knew the bay like the palms of their hands. No other men could have taken the boats so close to the uneven coast on a dark night.

Shunter and Finbar Daly stiffened when they saw the light blinking from the leading boat. A faint light that was quenched almost as soon as they saw it.

"Begod," said Shunter sitting up straight. "They're in it!"

All of the others came awake. They stood up, crouched, peering ahead. The pulses of all of them began to pound.

Bartley spoke to his son, John, who was lying full stretch on the small hatch at the bow. "It's about a hundred yards," his son said. Bartley handed the tiller over to the third man in the boat, a short stumpy man with a pipe perpetually in his gob, lighted or unlighted. They called him Mick McQuaid, on account of that. He took the tiller. "Turn her in time now," said Bartley, "or I'll crucify you." Then he crossed the hold and placed his body beside his son's. He raised his left hand, so that Mick could see it against the lightening sky. "When I drop it," said Bartley back to him, in a whisper, "turn her and drop the sail."

Mick took a firm grip on the tiller and wound the sail rope around his arm. It dug in deep so he swelled the tendons to bear the strain.

Bartley looked behind him. He could make out Melia's boat a good twenty yards away and barely see the other boats closing up on them. The trawler was a long, squat shape ahead. There were no lights burning on her. They would all be hidden behind heavy cloth. He could see the ugly bow of her rising in front and the squat wheelhouse resting on her tail. She was heading very slowly toward the southwest, almost into the wind. They could hear the chugging of the slowly turning engine. So she was trawling a seine net. That would hold up her speed appreciably. He moved his left hand gently and Mick eased the boat over in that direction. The boat cut across almost into the west so that they would shortly cross the trawler's course.

Nearer now, Bartley could see the shape of a man's head in

the wheelhouse, lighted by the binnacle light. He crouched lower. There was very little sound from their own boat. It would be covered by the noise of the slowly turning engine.

He rose to his knees. His son rose beside him, levering up the long pole with the steel hook on the end of it. They closed on the trawler. Bartley had his hand raised, about to drop it when, clear and distinct, carried by the wind over the sound of the boats and the sails and the chugging engine, there came the lively bark of a little dog. It was such a foreign sound in such a place that Bartley remained petrified. There was action on the trawler. A bulkhead door was thrown open and they saw two men coming out and peering over the side at them. Then they shouted and ran.

Bartley dropped his hand. Mick swung the boat in and let the sail rope run off his arm. Bartley cursed and cursed Melia's pup as he stood to his full height and reached for the side of the trawler. He gripped it. The trawler suddenly sprang away as if she had sat on a nest of ants, and Bartley was swept off the deck of his own boat, and his son was left foolishly standing up holding the long pole out to the air. Bartley hauled himself up. He was faced by figures. He struck out with his fists. A forlorn hope. He was off balance. He saw a raised arm and felt the crunch of something hitting his forehead. He thought he saw the carnival lights in the Square in the middle of Race Week and then the cold water closed over his head.

Melia had hushed his dog. If he wasn't a kind man he would have wrung his neck. He had seen the action ahead. He had swung his boat on the track of Bartley's, but he was too late for the trawler. He only got a blast of air from her as her stern passed by. But in passing he saw the form of Bartley clinging to her sides and he saw him falling in an unlovely sprawl into the sea and he did a very strange thing. He raised the pup high and he flung it toward the sinking body of Bartley. Then he tried frantically to turn the boat, but, of course, she only stalled. The sails flapped idly and he had to swing away on a wide tack to come back on the spot where Bartley had fallen.

That poor pup was very surprised. How could this strange new individual it had found be so cruel? The water took it and shook it and soaked it and it emerged and it whined and barked very indignantly, since water is no place for a terrier, and when Bartley's head emerged from the sea and he saw a small barking and crying dog in line with his eyes, he nearly gave up the ghost and died there and then, because, God knows, this bloody dog had been haunting him and was the cause of all his misfortune. But he stretched a hand weakly and took hold of the thing and wrapped it round his neck, and the dog started licking the side of his face. "Oh, you son of a bitch," said Bartley naming the thing well. He flapped his arms in the water, trying to keep himself on top of it like a man climbing a cock of hay. He let out one shout and then he roared at the dog. "Bark, you bastard! Bark, can't you?" and with two tough fingers he pinched the pup on the behind.

The pup howled.

And that was how Shunter swept in and stuck a hook in Bartley before the weight of his sea boots and his woollen jerseys and his heavy coat brought him down forever to the bottom of the sea.

Shunter's boat was first home and they climbed out of it and they waited for Melia to come in, with Bartley standing up tall in the dawn light, dripping-wet, holding a bedraggled pup in one hand and dabbing at the wound on his forehead with the other, and Shunter sitting on a bollard, stuffing a pipe with great satisfaction and quietly waiting for the show to begin.

The Boy and the Brace

‣<o>‣

T HE DRUM SPOKE first. "Come on, come on, come on, come on!" it boomed; and with crahs and crangs and peeps and bommoms the other instruments, encouraged, answered, and the band swung from the big square of the town into the mouth of the street, the tall buildings taking the shocking impact of sound, leaning away from it and deflecting it into the blue sky.

It was a warm somnolent day and save for the listless spread-eagled dogs the street was almost deserted. A few bored-looking shop assistants deigned to stroll to their doorways, to lean there with folded arms and watch with some sympathy the members of the band, who were puffing and blowing and sucking, excited momentarily by this audience for their windy gymnastics; forgetting the sweat gathering in armpits, backs and legs, thinking what heroes they were to come out on a day like this, and for what? For voluntary and, even worse, unpaid, except maybe for a pint of porter later whose froth would be only a shadow of its true glory after the deflating heat of the day.

But this was our band and we were proud of it, proud of little Padneen, who was called Sucker because he played the big horn; and long, thin Gaeglers, who played the fife – the customary crack from the loungers at the Four Corners was for him to be careful or he might fall into it. Upsetting remarks like that served to break the rhythm of our band and caused strange angry noises to emanate from the bassoon. For we were not proud of our band in an open boastful sort of way but in a jeering, sneering sort of way which was a cloak for the real affection we felt for all its members. Even foreigners would have to admit that the band played with great verve and marched in time and, like all amateurs, the men loved their work; and as you stood and listened, little chills ran up your spine and you thought: Ah, they are great lads, so they are! A credit to the town they are! And you would purse your lips and emit a resounding razzberry or shout an insult to cover the fact that you were becoming emotional.

The kids absolutely adored the band, every blow and puff and suck of it. All they wanted was the hint of sweet music merged with a strong cacophony of sound and they would flock.

They flocked now!

Like rabbits from burrows they came. At the top of the winding street – no children to be seen. You'd think the citizens hadn't been procreative for a thousand years. Then suddenly – a thousand children, pushing and shoving and screeching and dancing. They fell on the band like bombs, causing confusion for a time. The big-drummer falling on his instrument and cursing loudly. The trombone player hitting a small skull with the slide out. Another drummer kicking a howling mongrel in the belly. Many things like that. But order was restored when the leader came from the front and knocked dust from a few backsides with his long and gaily decorated baton.

In order then once more, the band proceeded down the winding street, garlanded and almost smothered in children, who took long steps and marched and chattered and sang, their faces red and shining and their hearts pumping fast with excitement.

The head of the procession was shortly taken by a tallish, well-built youth who strutted ahead, swinging an imaginary baton, his body forming an arc as he pushed out his chest. His hair was of an indeterminate colour because it had been clipped almost to the bone by his father; none of it remaining after the hygienic scalping except a forelock that flapped to his antics. His shirt was in its first day and hence clean, and the trousers, held up by a length of twine, were whole everywhere but at the back, where his shirttail had worn its way through. His exposed parts were burned nut-brown by the sun, and you knew his name was Mico because on all sides of him were admiring youngsters, encouraging him in his gyrations, shouting: "Ah, jay, Mico! Mico is gass, isn't he? Look 't um!" Mico expanded in it.

The band leader made a few ineffective attempts to dislodge his usurper, but in vain. Mico was fleet of foot and always returned. So they passed from one winding street of tall houses to another winding street of not-so-tall houses, and the drum boomed, fingers fiddled and lungs blew. A brave sight it was, and the noise woke the old town from summer somnolence.

"Dum, dum, dum, dum, dum-ditty-dee, dum-dum," cried the band, swinging into the introductory phrase of the well-known march. The kids instinctively waited for the correct beat and then they roared, parodying the heartbreaking melody:

> "Oh, all of a sudden
> A lump 'f black pudden
> Came floating through the air!"

And they danced as they sang, hopping on their brown legs and swinging their arms and tripping over mongrels, and Mico outdid himself in his body contortions and the vein at the side of his neck swelled to the bursting point as he took the tune an octave higher than the others just to show that he was the boss. They swung into another narrow street and halfway along there was an opening into another long street, which went away from the sun.

On either side this street was bounded by two-storey half-bricked houses with their doorsteps right on the narrow paths flanking the macadam. They were nice houses and you knew from the appearance of them that their owners were poor and maybe honest, but clean in the main, because the curtains behind the windowpanes were of white starched lace shown off by a bowl of the inevitable geraniums.

The street was remarkable for only one thing: that was the figure of the small boy who stood in the center of it, halfway up and watching from his distance the colourful conglomeration passing him below. His hair was red and his eyes were blue and his face was very pale. Everybody knows that people with red hair have pale complexions if they haven't very red ones. There is no in-between with red hair. But even allowing for that, the boy's face was much paler than Nature had intended it to be. The face was thin and the shoulders in the red gansey were narrow. It was only when you allowed your eyes to travel down that you noticed the heavy bandage where the kneecap should have been and the steel brace with the bright new straps. You understood then, perhaps, why he was so thin and looked so pale.

It was one of Mico's junior satellites who drew his attention to the figure in the street, just before the band had passed by the opening.

"Mico! Mico!" he screamed. "It's Joe! Lookit Joe! He's out! They musta let 'm out!"

Mico glanced at him. He couldn't hear. "What is it, Snitch?" he asked, his hand to his ear.

Snitch, despairing of making himself understood by word of mouth, pointed frantically to the fast disappearing opening. Mico screwed his head around to take a look, spotted the figure of Joe and left the procession with a leap.

"Hey, fellas," he roared, "it's Joe! Joe is back!" And he dived into the throng, promptly followed by seven or eight of his fellows. The band watched their departure with relief in their eyes, and as they passed on, you could almost hear a sigh of relief being squeezed from the instruments.

Joe, his eyes shining a little, was soon surrounded by boys; by Mico, taller than any of them except poor, skinny Joe, and Snitch the smallest of them, his jerseyed arm rising constantly to wipe a freely running nose. Then Pakey, Padneen, and John Willie, the three brothers whose eventual death on the gallows was predicted by harassed parents in the neighbourhood; and Yank, so called because he still wore the trousers of a sailor suit which a fond aunt in America had sent him for Christmas; and a small, very fat boy known as Dripping for obvious reasons.

All talking at once they were: "Jay, Joe, what did they do t'y'? Whin did they let y' out, Joe? Jay, Joe, look at the yoke on the leg! What's it for, Joe? Jay, isn't it a wonder?"

Joe felt good. It seemed a long time ago that he had gone to hospital. It was only six months, but it was like that many years. He had been the leader of them then, with Mico number two. Now Mico was the big noise. But Joe didn't mind. Just to be out again. To see them. Their faces excited with seeing him. It was great. It was all past. The pain in the knee that he couldn't understand; going to hospital with fear in his heart — he had seen so many people from the street going to that hospital, and the next thing you were walking behind them and they stiff in wooden boxes being carried in a hearse with the horses in front and white yokes around their necks and their hoofs polished. He had been waiting all the time to be carried out in the wooden box so that when they told him they would have to take off his kneecap and after that he would be all right, he didn't mind. Anything at all, so that he wouldn't die and not see the fellas any more.

He was as good as new now. Just that it was a bit of a nuisance to have your leg in the brace, so that you couldn't run very fast, or walk very fast for that matter. It was funny to think that you would never have a knee like other fellas, that your leg would never bend in the middle again, but it didn't matter now, with the fellas around him. It was worth it all to see them. Forget the pain in the white bed and the smell of stuff all around you that never went away, so that even the scent of the flowers outside seemed to be tainted with it. Now, with the sun shining out of the blue sky and the fellas all around asking questions and carrying on, what did it all matter? Divil a thing really.

He walked about a bit to show them how the brace worked.

"See the way it's stuck into the heel of the boot, fellas," he pointed out. "It comes up ta here on your leg and y' strap it. See!" He pulled up the leg of his trousers to show it to them.

"Jay" and "Jayney" and more colourful words issued from them in a splurge of admiration and envy. "Jayney, isn't it well for you, Joe?" Mico said with his voice wistful. "None at all of the fellas this side of the town has a brace. Have yeh no knee at all, Joe?"

"No," said Joe proudly. "They cut off me knee altogether."

"Jaykers!" they chorused again.

"Walk about a bit'll we see it workin', Joe," suggested Mico.

So Joe took his steps, having to lift the brace a little in the air and swing it in a circle to get his bad leg ahead of the other. They were thrilled with this and proceeded to imitate him, stiffening one leg at the knee and swinging it in a semi-circle. The band, whose music had faded into the distance, was forgotten as they went around in a ring after Joe.

But Joe suddenly felt very tired, and the sweat which broke out on his forehead was cold, so he stretched his bad leg in front of him and sat on the edge of the hot concrete path. They squatted around him and plied him with questions. Was it bad havin' his knee cut off? No, it wasn't, because they put a yoke over your kisser and you breathe in and you go to sleep and when you wake up the job's done, and there y'are. After, it's a bit sore. What did he get to eat? Was it good stuff or bad stuff? Oh, good! Eggs and milk and every day a sweet after dinner. A what after dinner? A sweet — y'know, the sort of stuff big shots have, red jelly in a sort of saucer plate and white stuff with it that melted in your mouth. Jay, imagine that! And apples and oranges every day near, and fellas in the ward with him that made him presents of this and that, sweets and chocolate and things. Oh, terrifico! Jay, they wished they had to go to hospital and get their knees cut off and get jelly and the white stuff and all the other rackets. And a grand steel brace at the end of it all. All for nix, too.

Joe felt very good. He hadn't been expecting this at all. Here he was a sort of hero to be envied, and he half expecting to be a bit jeered at, as a sort of unfit person who was defective in the body. He knew from experience in this neighbourhood what it meant to have weak eyes, say. "Four eyes," you were called, and they would pinch your steel-framed glasses and jeer at your fumbling around to find them, and when they had reduced you to weak tears you would get them back again. If your legs were defective you would be called "Hoppity," and if you had a squint you would be called "Gunner." Now, here he was, his fears laid at rest, the hero of the hour, and the fellas practically jealous of the evil that had befallen him.

Half an hour at least they were sitting there, closely questioning him and surmising and telling him the news of things they had done since he went away, and then faintly in the distance could be heard the sound of the band returning from the parade.

It was Snitch was the first to notice it.

"Whist, lads," said he, stopping the talk. "Is that the band comin' back again?"

They listened.

"That's it, all right," said Pakey.

"Are they goin' t' come back the same way?" Yank asked.

"Sure," said Mico, "they always do. Don't they, Joe?"

"They always did," said Joe, picturing to himself hearing the band at home when he might be sitting down to his tea, maybe, stuffing bread and jam into his mouth, and he would swallow off the scalding tea, his mother berating him and saying: "Time enough, time enough you'll be out to see the damn' band. Eat your bread slow! Drink your tea slow! You'll end up with a bad stomach like your father, so you will!" But he wouldn't have the patience to finish anything. He'd be out the door and flying down the street, twisting around the corner, chewing the last bit, and out of the other houses the other kids would be coming, stuffing their mouths, roaring through it, "Hi, Joe, wait for me, Joe, wait for me!" But Joe couldn't wait. He was very fleet and he'd always be the first there to join the band or watch a dogfight or a man fight or two cats fighting on a tin roof.

A restlessness came over the boys as the strains of the band became louder and louder. Joe could feel it and he could feel his own heart thumping. They all rose to their feet and instinctively turned their heads toward the end of the street where at any moment the band would appear. Then Snitch started running without a word. You couldn't blame Snitch in a way. He was so small that he had to have a good head start of the others if he wanted to end up anywhere near them.

"Hi, Snitch!" Mico yelled, but Snitch just dug his chin deeper into his neck and ran on.

"After'm, fellas!" roared Padneen, taking the lead.

The others whooped and chased after Padneen. All except Mico.

"Hey, what about Joe?" Mico yelled after them.

They paid not the least attention.

Mico looked at Joe.

"Come on, Joe, run!" he said.

"All right, Mico," said Joe, lifting his braced leg and swinging it in a semicircle. He hopped a few steps at a fast pace. Mico, ahead of him, half turned, running sideways, looking back at him. Joe halted. He felt his heart thumping and he knew his face was paler.

"Run, Joe, run!" said Mico more urgently, sensing the imminent appearance of the band.

"All right, Mico," said Joe, starting up again. A few steps at a fast pace.

"That's it, Joe," Mico encouraged him. "Faster! Faster!"

Joe stopped. His strained eyes looked at Mico and there was an appeal in them.

"I can't, Mico," said Joe, "I can't run."

"You can, a course," said Mico, still moving away, turning his head to see how close the band might be. "Come on, Joe, you can do it, so you can!"

Joe just stood there in the centre of the road and shook his head.

"Ah, come on, Joe, for God's sake!" said Mico impatiently. He looked toward the end of the street. The head of the band parade was already appearing around the corner. Mico gave Joe a last look. "Are y' comin', Joe?" he asked, and then he turned his head away finally and bolted down the street.

Mico's back became smaller and smaller, as Joe watched. He saw the mouth of the street being filled with the bodies of the children, and the sun reflecting blindingly from the polished instruments. He saw the tall figure of Mico pressing and pushing until he had reached the head of the procession, where he arched his body and swung an imaginary baton.

The noise and the hoots and the cheers and the singing passed by and left only the echo behind them.

Joe stood there a little longer and then he sat painfully on the path. He was alone. He couldn't check the hotness behind his eyes, the empty feeling in his wasted body. He pressed the palms of his almost transparent hands into the sun-heated pavement and he prayed desperately. Very deep inside himself with his eyes tight shut, he prayed: "Please, Jesus Christ, don't let them call me Hoppity. Please don't let them call me Hoppity."

The River

THE RIVER ROSE out of the lake that drained the great mountains.

They were very tall, stern-looking mountains. They surrounded the lake and kept the shine of the sun from it for the greater part of the day so that it looked gloomier than it was and rather sad. It was high up and, once the river left it, it seemed to become exceedingly jolly as it ran out of the shadow of the mountains.

First it was wide and deep and placid, but as it started to fall on its ten-mile journey to the sea, it narrowed and twisted and foamed and fell and threw up banks of yellow sand where salmon loved to lie. As it got nearer to the coast, it cut its way through tall gorges of rock and it fell over high falls until, in places, it was a rippled foam-laced interruption cutting the bleak plain, where cattle discontentedly eat at the sparse grass of the poor soil. The nearer it got to the sea, the greater its fall, and here, there were high, rounded hills that were very fertile. Trees grew on the hills and they were subdivided and looked green and pleasant under the sun with white cottages built between the fields, and way out beyond you could see great stretches of silver sand where the sea would wink bluely or greyly under the direction of the sky.

And here, a few hundred yards from the estuary, the river was glorious. It fell over a twenty-foot fall in an eternal rumble that never ceased. Many people would walk down to gaze at it there, and you'd think the river knew it was an object of admiration and awe. There were pools above the fall and pools below the fall and it was very natural that apart from the people who went to admire, there were also people there with long rods in their hands, whose purpose was to catch the powerful fish waiting below to jump the falls or as they rested above, after their supreme accomplishment. Foolish people who really didn't care about eating salmon would spend hours watching them leaping there; to see the powerful fins catch hold in the white strength of the water, grip it and move the powerful tails and swim up and up and up until they vanished at the top of the fall with a disdainful and triumphant flick of their tails. Some of them did not succeed. Sometimes they left a smear of scales and red blood on an outcropping black rock.

But the river was good for a show, either way.

Twenty yards from the falls there was a road that went down to the sea, and by the side of the road there was a two-storey house surrounded by a garden that held many spring flowers, and in this house, in a certain room in it, a telephone was ringing. Nothing could be more incongruous than the difference between this occurrence and the river. It was a square room with shelves all around the walls and a long, wooden table and forms and notices hanging up about such things as dipping sheep and precautions against the warble fly and notices faded and yellow with small print that few people could take time out to read. A tall young man dressed in the blue uniform of the Civic Guards came in and took up the phone. His tunic collar was opened and a cigarette hung from the corner of his mouth. He looked sleepy. He took up the phone and said, "This is the Barracks," and such a barking and sizzling proceeded to come from the instrument that the young policeman pulled the cigarette from his mouth and dropped it on the floor and ground it with his heel, and then started to button up his tunic. His only words of conversation were: "Yes, sir. Yes, sir. Yes, sir."

Then he placed the phone back on the table reverently, emitted a cautious sigh and went quickly out of the room. He ran upstairs on the double and knocked at a door from which the sound of singing was coming, entered on a grunt and said, "Sergeant, it's the chief superintendent on the phone and he's leppin'."

The sergeant looked at him from the middle of a soap-covered face. He was wearing trousers and a shirt. His hair was scanty and stood on top of his head. He was a big man wearing a comfortable stomach and blue eyes that were filled with humour.

"Leppin' is he?" the sergeant asked.

"Mad," said the young man.

"Hum," said the sergeant. "What have we done wrong, Moloney?"

"Divil a thing, Sergeant," said Moloney. "What the hell could we do wrong here?"

"The only safe place to say a thing like that," remarked the sergeant, "is a place called hell. All right. I'll go down and listen to the man."

He didn't hurry himself down the stairs. The young police-man walked impatiently behind him. He was boiling with curiosity. It was such a small place they were. Nothing ever happened. Nobody seemed to know they were even in the place. Moloney felt sometimes that people would know more about them if they were in the middle of a desert. For a chief superintendent to call them up was really something big.

The sergeant took up the phone and sat at the table.

"This is the sergeant," he said.

The phone started barking at him.

Moloney knew that the news wasn't pleasant because the sergeant didn't answer back at all. He just rested his big, half-unshaven face in his hand, listened closely and looked out over the land through the open window. It was obvious that the man at the end of the phone would leave space for an answer, probably in the affirmative. But there would be no answer so he would go on. Eventually he had to run out of words. The yapping was silent, then barked an exasperated query to which the sergeant gave a slow and considered, "Yes" – a long pause and then, "Chief superintendent," and put down the phone on the rest. He put both his elbows on the table, and chewed at his knuckles with the nice white teeth that weren't his own. He saw where the waters of the land and sea meet at the estuary and the very white houses along the line of the winding road, and the neat green fields and the reeks of turf piled up.

"That bloody river," said the sergeant.

Moloney was hopping from one leg to another.

"Well, what was it, Sergeant? What did he want?"

"Moloney," the sergeant questioned him, "is this a bad village?"

"It is not," said Moloney, "more's the pity. Aren't they all like redblooded saints except on St Patrick's night?"

"Am I liked in the village, Moloney?" asked the sergeant.

Moloney considered this.

"Well, considering everything, Sergeant," said Moloney, "I think so."

"So we have a respectable village where the police are popular," said the sergeant. "Do you think this happened overnight, Moloney?"

"I don't suppose it did," said Moloney.

"How right you are," said the sergeant. "I'm here twenty-three years and if the place is like it is now it's me that med it that way, and I med it that way because I used a bit of me thinkin' apparatus. Listen, Moloney, you have all them philosophers writin' books. If I could write a book about this psychology stuff I'd make a holy show of them fellas. Do you know that?"

"Listen, Sergeant," Moloney burst out. "What the hell did he want?"

The sergeant ignored him. He rose, went to the window and leaned out on the sill through the open window, his balding head in the sunshine.

"And now that goddamed river has to spoil everything," he said. "Look at it, tumbling its way into the sea, and because of it I have to destroy the hard-thinking work of twenty-three years and have them all again pulling down blinds over their eyes when we meet together on the road."

"I have it," said Moloney joining him. "It's about the fishing."

"Yes," said the sergeant. "The river got a new owner lately. You saw him. He kem in here to tell us that any more if we wanted to fish we'd have to give him half of everything we caught. You remember him, a small, sawed-off piece of parasite that never did a day's work in his life with two thin lips on him like a knife slit in skinny bacon. He's been places, that little man, though you'd wonder how the bird's legs he has would carry him that far. Yes, he's seen the chief and he's written to the castle and the Dáil and the Taoiseach and Dublin Castle and the upshot is that they say we are not cooperating with the worthy owner of the fishery, that too many salmon are leavin' by the back door and that he wants action and they want action. Everybody wants action. I had it all worked out. I know how many fish were leavin' the river. Not a lot. Just enough. They all knew me. I'd put up with a certain amount, they knew. Now I strike. What happens? Forty times the fish will leave the river and what happens to the village. It will become contrary. I know. They don't know. They don't give a goddam. I've built this village. I've reared it like a mother, and now I have to destroy what I built in a night over that little —"
He banged down the window and sat on the form.

"Why didn't you explain it to the chief superintendent?" Moloney asked.

"You're young," said the sergeant. "You'll learn."

"I see," said Moloney doubtfully.

"So tonight," said the sergeant, "we go after Mickey."

"But, Sergeant," said Moloney, "Mickey is your best friend."

"I know," said the sergeant. "That's why." He looked into Moloney's wide-puzzled eyes.

There was a bright moon that night.

"You stay here," said the sergeant to the water bailiff. The sergeant disliked the man. He had sandy hair and prominent teeth so he always seemed to be sneering.

The sergeant wanted to say to him, "If only you did your job right all this wouldn't be happening." Which was hardly fair. Sandy tried hard but one night about ten years ago when he was really trying he ended up in a deep pool in the river and had never shown the same enthusiasm for the job. "If he sees you, it's all up. Come on," he said to Moloney.

The sergeant had an old raincoat buttoned up around him and an old hat on his head. He went along the favourite side of the river with a short stick in his hand. In the deceptive light it looked like a gaff. He would pause at each pool and he would get down on his stomach as if he were examining the lies. Then he would rise and meander on. He cursed frequently under his breath. He felt very bitter. His heart was heavy. He could see the train of inevitable things that would happen after tonight. After this they would want an army with heavy artillery to keep the whole village away from the river. And they were so blind and stupid that they couldn't see it.

He knew exactly where Mickey would be. And Mickey was there. He knew that Mickey had spotted his manoeuvring. Mickey could see a single horsefly in the middle of an alder bush. The only thing that would puzzle him would be the identity of the amateur poacher. The sergeant kept up his wandering getting closer and closer to the Priest's Pool. It was a pleasant place where the river wound. On the far side, there was a yellow gravel beach. This side, the river flowed free and by reclining on the thick grass you could caress the water with your fingers. Mickey was lying stretched there, only his eyes appearing over the edge. He was looking at something in the water. His hand was held by his side. Any minute now the sergeant knew, that right hand would flash and a glittering, contorted fish would be rising helplessly in the air.

The sergeant rose up.

Mickey saw him. He signalled him down.

"You fool! You fool!" Mickey said to him in a harsh whisper. "Keep your shadow off the pool."

The sergeant instinctively ducked, and then rose up and threw away the hat, opened the coat and threw that away.

"I don't know who you are," said the sergeant, "but I arrest you for the illegal procuring of salmon on another man's river."

He saw the amazement on Mickey's face. It was a pleasant face. Black, virile hair even though he was nearing fifty, a burned face seamed with laughter wrinkles all over it and blue eyes. He always wore faded brown clothes. They merged better. Amazement on his face, and incredulity. Is this the man I sit and talk with for hours into a morning, while we sip beer and smoke too many cigarettes, and arrange the world between us – what's wrong with politics and religion and the country's youth?

He saw a protest forming on Mickey's open mouth. A protest or something. Was he going to call me Brutus, wondered the sergeant? Then Mickey threw the gaff on the ground and turned away. There Moloney rose up to face him. Mickey saw the buttons gleaming in the moonlight and then he turned back and the sergeant knew he was leppin'.

There was only one way to break free. The sergeant blocked the way, so Mickey threw himself on the sergeant.

I'm an old man, the sergeant thought, as he felt the power of the smaller man in his arms. Squirming like an eel, flicking his body like a powerful fish leaping the waterfall. They fell to the ground clasped in a sweaty embrace. For a moment on the ground they faced each other. The sergeant was the stronger man. There was sadness in his eyes. They looked at each other. Now is the time for him to spit out a curse and a name at me, thought the sergeant. To his horror, Mickey just shook his head, released his grip and relaxed.

At that moment the sergeant threw the chief superintendent out of the window.

"Hit me, Mickey, for God's sake," he said.

Mickey was quick. He hit him.

You'd hear the sergeant groaning over in the next four counties. He rolled on the ground, and sat up, holding his head while Mickey was up and away like a shadow. Moloney came.

"Are you hurtit?" he wanted to know.

"I'm dying," said the sergeant.

"I got a look at him," said Moloney. "I'd know him agin. He ran into the first house up on the road."

"You'll get promotion out of this, Moloney," said the sergeant bitterly.

"Where's that moron of a water bailiff?" he asked then.

"He's twenty yards away on a hill lookin' at us, Sergeant," said Moloney.

"He would," said the sergeant, staggering to his feet. Then in a loud voice, "After him, Moloney. We'll get him now on a double charge." He limped after Moloney. They came to the house. There was no light in it. The sergeant looked back. Sandy was behind them, watching. The sergeant banged on the door. "Who lives here?" the sergeant asked.

"I don't know, Sergeant," said Moloney.

"Well, there's one thing sure," said the sergeant. "We can't break into any man's house without a search warrant. That's the law. It may be a bad law, but it's the law and that's all that's to it. I'll go and get the search warrant and you stand guard here at the front door.

"But what about the back door, Sergeant?" Moloney asked. "Couldn't someone slip out the back while I'm watchin' the front?"

"That's a good thought, Moloney," said the sergeant. He called then in a loud voice to the water bailiff. "Here, you! Come and stand guard at the back door, and hurry up or your man will have slipped out the back while you're comin'. How can I catch poachers when I get no cooperation?" He said this in a loud voice. Sandy came running. "Ye nearly caught him, all right," he said. "But he's holed up proper now."

"Go to the back door," said the sergeant, "and stay there until mornin' if you have to. I'll have to rouse a justice of the peace for a search warrant but I'll be back as soon as I can and we'll grab him." It's a good job, he was thinking, that Sandy is as dumb as a bucket of water. "On guard now, min," he said to them, "and don't let him out of yeer sight. I'll collect the evidence below at the river and I'll be back."

He walked away from them to the river bank. He was humming a bit. He was thinking, Well, to hell with it, I'm nearly pensioned off, anyhow, as it is. He picked up the gaff where it had dropped in the struggle. He went to walk off, started and paused. What had Mickey been looking at? Well, it doesn't matter. He walked on. Then he walked back. I'll just look, anyhow. He got down on his belly and peeped over the edge. He whistled softly. Great God, he must be up to twenty-five pounds! He was beautiful. It was the moon betrayed him. He was motionless in the clear water. A small head and a round body on him. Beautiful. That's the way, said the sergeant. His heart was pounding. He rose to his knees. I may as well get back. He used the gaff to get himself to his feet.

The gaff. The sergeant looked at the wicked winking point of it. Terrible things, terrible things, man.

He got back on his belly. He looked once. He struck. Something jolted his arm as if he had hold of an exploding hand grenade. Great God! The eyes were bulging out of his head. His heart was turbulent. Full of triumph, and a great fear that somehow he was going to lose the beautiful creature.

He started to pry him loose from the water.

A soft voice from his right-hand side, tsked, and tsked.

"What's the country comin' to?" the voice asked. "Corruption in high places. Bloody poachers in the police force. And amateur poachers, at that," went on the voice urgently, as the salmon started to play the sergeant.

"For the love of God help me, Mickey," said the sergeant, "or he'll get away."

The King

——— ◦ ———

I SAW THE King three times in all. The first time we were endeavouring to rob him. It was our custom during the proper season to adjourn to the small market place where the country people came on a Saturday to sell their eggs and fowl and turf and odds and ends. Always great colour there and confusion. Big women in shawls and red petticoats and heavy boots, and their men in bainin coats and ceanneasna trousers and the boots known as farmer's friends. The smell of porter and horses and asses and potatoes fresh from pits and eggs hot from hens and the yellow pats of butter wrapped in cabbage leaves. Loud talk and braying and waving of ashplants in brown hands and an optimistic street musician playing country songs that brought tears to leathery cheeks and hands to worn purses. The Small Crane they called it, and we loved it.

Daneen and Jojo and myself were in it this day. We were sadly in need of equipment to make bows and arrows. In such case all you had to do was to go to this place and when an ass cart swung out of the small square, with the bundles of sally rods tied together and dangling behind, you crept up and pulled at the ends and drew them forth before the owner was aware of his loss. They were grand and long. The thick end made the bow, and the top end, pointed and sharpened, was excellent for hitting and exploding the bulbs in the electric light standards.

So we dodged and laughed and jeered behind their backs at the Irish-speaking countrygoms. We were very swift at this time because it was summer and we wore just torn shirts and trousers and our bare feet. We patted the noses of the hay-eating horses and pulled the tail of an ass to see could we tell what the weather would do, Daneen having one in his house, a small yoke of a toy ass with a string tail that could tell what the weather was going to do from the feel of it. The real ass didn't. Jojo spotted the cart leaving the place.

"Hi, they's one now, fellas," Jojo roared pointing at the ass cart with the tips of the bundled sally rods waving behind.

"Get after 'm, in the name a God," said Daneen spitting on his palms and rubbing them together as was his custom before action.

We jinked our way after the ass cart. Many people turned and cursed at us, mainly in Irish, which we didn't understand at this time, so that we weren't in the least offended. Under horses' bellies we went too, so that they reared up after we had passed and the owners' faces got red as they tried to quieten them, and we came up on the back of the home-going cart like panthers, bending down and our thin hands reaching up. Daneen, who was great at things like this, got the first one. It was a dandy. One great bow and two arrows at least. It would cause great destruction. Jojo pulled next and got one too. It was passable. Then I pulled and of course something went wrong and I nearly pulled the cart off the ass's back, so that the owner, who was sitting in front, turned and saw us and reached back with the whip and aimed a blow at me. He was successful. I felt the sting of it and it made me mad.

"You bloody oul bogman!" I shouted at him, rubbing my cheek, furious that I had failed.

He said a lot of things then. In Irish. They must have been bad because they twisted his face. He was a strong-looking man with great muscles in his bare neck. I can always remember his face this time, and the other two times too for that matter. A strong face wanting a shave with bristles heavy on it and a moustache creeping down the sides of his mouth making him look like a picture of Genghis Khan in the history book, curse it, at school. His teeth were pointed and very white and he had thick eyebrows that jutted out over his eyes. They were very blue and not stern-looking, mind you. Even while he was cursing me I liked the look of him. He could be someone that you'd say would be great gas.

"Countrygawk, countrygawk, countrygawk!" I blatted at him like a music machine.

He alighted from the cart then and came back waving the whips. We backed away. I backed away first. Then I heard Daneen.

"Jay!" Daneen was ejaculating with awe. "It's the Potheen King, lads. It's the Potheen King."

That stopped us. For wasn't he a hero? There were more stories about him that could write two books and leave some over afterwards. We were all brought up on tales of him, of his utter cleverality in outwitting the hated policemen. I can't tell you all of them. Just about how he would get potheen past battalions of them. Even when they searched his cart and his ass and his wife and himself and his loads of turf. The potheen always arrived at its destination. Didn't he even arrange a great funeral one time and got enough through to drunken the whole of the county Galway? Oh, he was a hero. Even when the English police went and the Irish ones came, he made hares of them, and to us in those days anybody who could do that to the police was the knees of the bees. He was the ultimate. Anyhow, what I want to be understood is that he was a hero to us all. So what do we do?

I say, "I'm sorry, King," I say. "Honest to God I didn't know it was you."

"Here," says Daneen holding out the stolen sally rod. "Have it back, King."

"I'll give you mine too," says Jojo, a little reluctantly.

"Give's a sup a potheen," says Daneen, very forward.

He laughs then, the King does, holding the oul ass by the reins. "Off with ye, ye scoundrels," he says. "Away with ye, ye poor misshapen city garsuns. Keep the oul bits of sticks and bedammed to ye."

That's all he said to us. Just that and he jumped up on the cart and drove away and we stood there looking after him admiringly. Once he turned and waved the whip at us, jollily, his white teeth shining.

"Jayney mac, isn't he great?" Daneen asked.

"That's really him?" I wanted to know.

"The very man," said Jojo.

We broke four electric light bulbs and my oul fella bet me.

The second time was a bit different. We were much older. We wore long trousers with good creases in them and we had oil in our hair, different smells on each so that if you passed us by you would think you were meeting a flower garden. We were sitting on the worn stones of the big town bridge trying to click with a few girls that might be passing out to Salthill. There was little doing. Probably because even though we were highly decorated we didn't look very prosperous. One look the lassies would give us that said plainly, Hair Oil and Happence, and off they passed us by, looking for better game, so that we were forced to shout insults after them.

"To hell with this," says Daneen then. "We'll go down and see an American wake. I'm goin' to be a celebis anyhow. I hate girls. Yah, yah, yah, they'd talk the leg off a pot, so they would."

"And spend pounds on you as well," said Jojo, who never saw a raw pound in his life that wasn't broken down into coppers and bobs.

I agreed. I liked American wakes. The big ships came to our bay at this time and all the young country people were going to America on them and it would make a cat laugh to see and hear all the wailing and caterwauling that went on down there.

We had a little difficulty in getting onto the dock where the tender was. The gatekeeper was a crusty old bird with a beard and a sailor suit and he wouldn't let his own mother past the gate unless she was legitimate. We had to use a subterfuge. A simple one that had worked before. A woman going in with a big crowd and showing the passes, so Jojo catches her shawl and Daneen catches Jojo's coat and then holds me by the hand and we cover our eyes with our arms and start bawling crying as if our hearts were going to break. We nearly brought concrete tears to the hard oul eyes of the gateman as we passed through.

The tender was about to pull away. It was packed with the emigrants. All clustered up at the back. A forest of handkerchiefs waving and red eyes all over the place. The shawled women on the quayside with their arms stretched out and the shawls trailing from their shoulders and the real tears pouring down their faces. The bainin men with the ashplants too, rubbing their noses with their fingers, choking it all back. It was a bit moving in a way if you let yourself become affected. So we didn't. We aped them a bit, and it would make you curl up to see Daneen with his arms held out and his face screwed up.

The tender hooted and spurted water and men threw off the ropes and she started to pull away from the quay.

It was then we saw the King.

He was standing with his arms spread out like Christ on the cross and he was crying. We hardly recognised him. He was old. His moustache was white even, and he had a red nose and he seemed to have withered a little. We weren't particularly keen on him now. Just a pleasant memory that we plucked up from the past.

"Why, that's the old King," said Daneen.

"As true as God it is," said Jojo.

We watched him.

He was a king in a way. He was kingly in that he saw his son going away on that tender and it was breaking his heart and he felt like crying aloud, so he cried and he didn't give a damn who saw him. He addressed his son too, in loving language. In Irish. We now knew some Irish. It had been forcibly impelled on us at school, the hard way. I knew what he was saying. He was saying:

"My jewel of a son, do not leave me! Do not leave your poor old father. I have nobody in the world now but you and my breast will be aching when you are gone. I will be left like a wren in an empty nest. Come back to me, my little white son, come back to me, do not leave me alone. My live eyes will never see you again. Let you leap the distance now between the big ship and the earth and come again to the weary arms of your faithful father." That's what he said. Between sobs and groans and the streaming tears. I saw his red-eyed son on the ship, looking so miserable with the cardboard suitcase at his feet. Big like his father had been. Out of place in his clothes and his shifting discomfort.

The boat pulled away and the son's hands tightened on the rail and from the ship and the quay there arose a crying like hundreds of curlews. We weren't jeering any longer somehow. We were quiet. You felt that there was a lot of real sorrow. The ship pulled away, the water churned into white porridge by the propellers, and when it was ten feet from the wall the King leaped after it with his hands outstretched.

He didn't reach it.

He fell into the white foam.

I saw the staring eyes of his son and I saw the life buoy thrown by one of the dockmen and I saw another man with his coat off, diving into the water. I saw the King coming to the surface, still wearing his cap with the peak down over his face. It was easy to see that he could not swim. He didn't care. He waved his hand at the departing ship before he went down again. Then the swimming man reached him and threw the life buoy over him.

The others waited to see him taken out dripping. There was a lot of laughing, they tell me. It was great gas, they tell me. I didn't wait. I still remembered the King as he was, the fine strong man. I didn't want to hear them laughing.

The third time I saw him was the next afternoon. I was on the far side of the docks, watching the green water. The sea gulls were wheeling. The water of the docks was slicked with oil from the ships and the coal dust of the stilled carts. You could see orange peelings in the water and floating cigarette packets and an odd drowned dog. It wasn't very clean water. No dock water ever is. The thought of diving into it even on a hot day would repel you.

I saw the men in the rowing boat out in the middle of the docks pulling the grapple behind them. I saw it catch on something, strain, and I saw the men who were using the grappling hooks shout back over their shoulders. The oars were stilled and I saw the wet rope of the grapple come into the boat and then I saw the face of the King rising out of the water. For a moment he faced me, with his closed eyes. He had lost his cap and you could see his forehead was white where the sun never saw it for the cap. His hair was very grey and very scanty. I thought his face was very small, and high up on his white forehead there was a light blue mark.

The men rowed slowly towards the steps, the steps with the green slime on them. The grapple man held the coat of the King and hauled him after the boat. His head fell forward and it made a special wake of its own in the slimy water.

Someone had heard him splashing in. Late last night.

He must have come down to say a phantom farewell to a lost son. He must have. And he must have slipped and hit his head on the granite of the quay and he must have slipped in then. The quay was the last place that held the sight of his beloved son. So he had come again. He must have fallen in. He may have taken a few jars to dull the agony of his separation. He might have staggered. Anything like that might have happened. After all he was old, wasn't he? He wasn't the tall rangy man that had defied the police of two countries, for the love of it I would say. So he died like that. Pathetic you say.

I don't know.

Poetic I'd say, who had seen it all.

The King is dead, and there'll be no other. Not again. There could have been only one and he had no son to bear the crown.

I went home when they reached the steps, and my head was down.

Other Walter Macken books
from Brandon

The Bogman

An orphan returns from Dublin to live with his tyrannical grand-father in a small village in the country. Walter Macken paints a memorable portrait of the hard life of subsistence farming, of loveless arranged marriages, and of rebellion against suffocating social mores.

"Comic and touching by turn; the anecdotes glide as smoothly as summer streams; the farming scenes are vividly done; it is all skilfully told with excellent dramatic moments." *Spectator*

"Macken captures the isolation and poverty of the village – its closed attitudes, its frozen social mores... and its deeply unfor-giving nature." *Irish Independent Weekender*

ISBN 0 86322 184 X; paperback £5.95

Rain on the Wind

The dramatic story of the constant struggle of the people of a fishing community – a struggle with the sea, with poverty and with the political conservatism of post-independence Ireland. No other novelist has so successfully portrayed the "ordinary" people of the West of Ireland in the decades when "the heroes of yesterday became the politicians of today". Winner of the Literary Guild Award and the Book of the Month Club Award when it was originally published, *Rain on the Wind* is one of Macken's most powerful and best-loved novels.

"Full of dramatic and racy incident." *Guardian*

"A rarely beautiful book. Mr Macken's engaging skill as a story-teller is matched by his deep understanding and tender (but never sentimental) affection for his characters." *New York Times*

ISBN 0 86322 185 8; paperback £5.95

Quench the Moon

Quench the Moon tells an unvarnished story of Ireland in the 1940s, a country full of the contradictions of its newly won freedom.

It is the story of Stephen O'Riordan, from the wild, hard and beautiful land of Connemara, of his hopes and ambitions, and of his passionate and stormy love for Kathleen, sister of his bitter enemy.

"Where the writer knows and loves his country as Walter Macken does, there is warmth and life." *Times Literary Supplement*

ISBN 0 86322 202 1; paperback £5.95

Brown Lord of the Mountain

Donn is born to the now mythical role of the Lord of the Mountain, a remote community in rural Ireland, unmarked by the passage of time. But Donn longs for a wider kingdom. He deserts his bride, roams the world, fights in wars, is footloose – yet finds that he is homesick.

Sixteen years later he returns to take up the threads of his old life, to learn to love his afflicted daughter, and to bring progress to the neglected valley. Then, on a night of innocent festivity, a monstrous crime is perpetrated.

His kingdom violated, Donn dedicates himself to a terrible revenge that can only destroy the avenger as well as the hunted.

"Excellent." *Irish Press*

"Walter Macken's dramatic, almost mystical tale, with full-blown romantic hero, reveals his theatrical background. Macken knows his people and his places and his love of them shines through; this final work is a fitting tribute to them." *Cork Examiner*

ISBN 0 86322 201 3; paperback £5.95

God Made Sunday and other stories

In *God Made Sunday* Walter Macken shows his unique ability to fashion memorable fiction from the everyday lives of people in the west of Ireland, evoking a world dominated by the incessant demands of working the land and the sea. The passions, humour and pathos of life are richly represented against the backdrop of the living landscape of his native Galway.

ISBN 0 86322 217 X; paperback £5.95